Mostly Vampires and Faeries: Fantasies of a Creative Writing Teacher

By Edgar Washburn

Cover art by Germancreative

Author's Note

This book is a work of fiction. Names, characters, places, and incidents are products of the author's imagination or are used fictitiously. Any resemblance to actual events or locations or persons, living or dead, is entirely coincidental.

For Marsha, my loving (Sonnet 116 kind) wife

Table of Contents

Introduction   1
Tabloid Angel   3
Hero Sword   12
Empath   27
Rusty Spur   47
Purpose   58
Willow-Wood Box   68
Fey Fay   78
Super V   94
Raven and the Thugs at Lizzie's Diner   104
Paranormal Christmas   110
Sidhe   113
Totem   132
Guardian   148

Introduction

I taught middle and high school English for over a decade and a half. In creative writing units and electives, I liked to write along with my students so that I could model the process from start to finish. Also, I just really liked to write, especially fiction.

I wrote the stories in this collection over several years. Each of these selections contains some element of fantasy or the supernatural. The stories tend to be fairly short because they fit within the criteria of student assignments. Some changes were made in rewrites to fit my original vision as opposed to what I thought should go into examples for student writers. There are some situational repetitions in the stories because I never thought of them as a body of work: they were tools of the teaching trade. Knocking the wind out of characters by having them struck in the solar plexus is apparently something that I like to do. Also, faeries pass themselves off as humans quite a bit.

As a literature major and teacher, I have read a great deal of "respectable" literature, but my heart really lies with writers like Robert E. Howard, J. R. R. Tolkien, Raymond Chandler, John D. MacDonald,

Robert McCammon, Jim Butcher, and numerous others who produced "popular" literature. I use quotation marks because I don't really believe in the delineation between respectable and popular.

This is my training-wheels venture. I hope that you enjoy the stories.

"There ain't no such thing as angels, Lizzy," Rick said, tapping his middle and index fingers on the tabletop for emphasis.

"What would your mother say if she heard you talking like that, God rest her soul?" Lizzy feigned righteous piety, but she was obviously warming to the argument.

Rick and Lizzy sat at their peeling Formica-topped table with Paul and Mary, a couple from across the trailer park. They got together a couple of nights each week to have drinks and maybe to watch a movie.

Mary said, "I read an article just the other day about a woman in a car wreck that said she was saved by an angel!"

"Honey," Paul said with a sigh, "you can't go believing the stuff you read in *The Star*. It's all bull."

"Yeah, a vampire drank my cat and then turned into the neighbor's dog!" Rick said and clinked bottles with Paul.

Mary watched them chuckle with a look of good-natured suffering. Then, she remembered something, and her eyes went wide, and she gasped. "There was a story about a vampire just last week. It happened just over to Buffalo. There was these bodies. . ."

Paul interrupted her. "We ain't talkin' about vampires. We're talkin'' about angels."

Lizzy and Rick lived in The Linnett Court trailer park with their son Rick Jr. He was sometimes called Rick Jay but usually just Jay. Thirty-two trailers dotted the open park and were connected by a series of narrow dirt roads. The entrance to the park meandered down a slight slope from County Road 27. Next to the trailer park stood the Town Sheds where huge piles of sand, salt, and gravel were kept for road maintenance.

Jay sat in the corner with his drawing pad and a yellow Ticonderoga pencil. His tongue protruded slightly from the corner of his mouth, and his brows beetled in concentration as he struggled to make the wings look feathery.

Lizzy made a clucking sound with her tongue as though she were about to scold a child. "There're angels in the Bible. I know you know that 'cause we sat next to each other in Sunday school."

"Jeeze woman, just 'cause there're angels in the Bible don't mean that some woman that cracked her car up saw one. She probably came fresh from the booby hatch."

"Mah," said Jay from his corner. All eyes turned toward him. They had forgotten that he was there.

"Yeah Sweetie?" Lizzy asked.

"Doesn't it say in the Bible that an angel can kill ten thousand guys with one swing of his sword?"

"Where did you hear that?" Lizzy asked, not at all happy about that particular portrayal of angels.

"A kid at school said so," Jay answered but never took his eyes from his picture.

"I suppose so, honey. Why?"

"I don't think I can draw a sword that long," he said.

"Let Mama see your picture, darlin'," Lizzy said, holding out her hand.

The four adults examined the picture of an angel, muscled like a comic book hero. His huge wings were opened, and he held an unfinished, flaming sword in one hand. Jay was only nine years old, but none of the adults could have drawn so well.

"He kinda looks like that guy on all the romance book covers," said Paul as though he were delivering some great artistic insight.

"Fabio," said Mary. "No, the angel looks more manly. That Fabio is sort of. . ." She paused, searching for the proper word. She couldn't find one, so she settled for, ". . . kinda mamby pamby, like a European."

"He is European," said Lizzy. "I think he is anyway."

"But Mah, what about the sword?" asked Jay.

"Honey, it's not really true. It's just supposed to teach a lesson."

"Aha!" shouted Rick, slapping the table and making the bottles rattle. "You admit the angel stories in the Bible ain't even true!"

"That ain't what I said at all!" returned Lizzy indignantly.

"The article said that vampires. . ." began Mary.

"We ain't talkin' about vampires or that Fabio guy neither!" Paul interjected.

Jay took his picture and went to his room. His parents never listened to him. They just liked to talk to grownups. He felt too upset and restless to hang out inside, so he decided to play outside. He knew he should tell his parents, but he didn't care. They wouldn't miss him anyway.

The sun began to sink below the horizon in a blaze of reds and oranges. The air snapped with chill, but Jay's denim jacket and Alfred State College baseball cap kept him warm enough. He felt good being outside without permission, almost as though his defiance would teach his parents a lesson.

His eyes fell upon the huge pile of gravel at the town sheds. His dad had forbidden him to climb on it. He said it was dangerous. Jay couldn't see why. It's not as though he would get hurt falling off; everything kind of sloped down. His dad just wanted to ruin his fun like always, just so he could hang out with grownups like Paul and Mary.

He walked with purpose to the gravel pile and began to climb. He didn't expect the rocks to cascade over his feet and hands, but he sort of liked the feeling. Halfway to the top he was tired. He felt as though he slid back one foot for every two he climbed. After a sneezing fit caused by the stirred dust, he felt his first prickle of unease, but his annoyance with his parents and defiance of their rules drove him the rest of the way up.

At the top of the gravel pile Jay should have felt a sense of triumph, but his throbbing muscles, sweaty back, and raspy throat made him nervous. The gravel pile was not a perfect cone but sagged in the middle as though a divot had been taken out of it. After looking around for a moment, he turned to begin his decent. His right foot sank into the gravel as he pivoted on it.

Jay's heart jumped into his throat. He tried pulling his foot free by pushing off with the other. That foot sank as well. He gagged on his terror and thrashed about trying to free himself. He slid toward the interior of the gravel pile.

Before his slide had come to a stop, gravel covered him up to his stomach. He feared moving anymore but needed to be free. Only for a moment did he worry that his parents would be angry with him. After that moment, he screamed or would have if his throat hadn't been so constricted with dust and fear. A strangled gasp was the only thing that escaped his lips. He tried again and again to scream, but nothing more than a squeaking whistle issued from his opened mouth.

Buried almost up to his armpits in gravel, he was trapped. Tears cut clean tracks in the dust covering is face, and his heart slammed against his ribs like a frightened bird.

Jay sensed a presence before seeing anything. A cool mist dampened his brow and made a chill run down his spine. For a split second, he almost started thrashing again, but he controlled himself, remembering how he had gotten himself into his situation.

Suddenly, a man was standing before him. He heard no approach, and not a single stone was displaced.

The man wore heavy-soled black shoes, black jeans, and a denim jacket. His hair was white-blonde and long, and his skin shimmered in the dusk, pale as milk. He looked mean and amused as well.

He grinned without humor. "Hey kid, whacha doin'?"

Jay could only wheeze, his mouth opening and closing like a goldfish's.

"Little trouble, huh?" the man asked.

Jay nodded his head vigorously, hoping that this might still turn out well.

"Gee," the man smirked, "I bet if you move at all, you'll just sink to the bottom." He grinned his humorless grin and added, "buried alive." He brought his heavy shoe down on the gravel and caused a small avalanche of stone.

The betrayal that Jay felt appeared plainly in his eyes. Then, his expression turned to sad resignation. His voice was like rustling autumn leaves. "I thought you were an angel." He looked down at his gravel trap. "Like Michael."

Something happened to the man's sardonic expression for just a moment. First surprise, then weariness flitted across his features, almost too quickly to be seen.

"I'm no angel," he said.

"I know," Jay said.

The man smiled a bit sadly. Though he appeared to be twenty years old, that smile made him seem terribly old and terribly tired.

"What would Michael, the Arch Angel do?" the man asked.

Jay looked at him skeptically, visibly holding back hope. He'd thought only moments ago that this man might actually kill him. He decided to take the plunge.

"I think Michael would save me and say something to make me feel better," he said defiantly.

"I bet he would at that," said the man. "I'm not Michael. My name is Ramsey." He squatted and grabbed a handful of Jay's denim coat and lifted him with one hand as though he were a boy made out of balloons. "I'm normally not a nice person."

Ramsey smiled broadly showing elongated canines, and his eyes flashed like new dimes. He chuckled and leaped into the air, hauling Jay behind him. They landed like a whisper at the foot of the gravel pile.

Ramsey released Jay and pointed a black-taloned finger at his face. "Never speak of this to anyone." Jay thought something in the bestial face looked embarrassed. "I'll know if you do."

Jay nodded wildly. "Okay," he said and crossed his heart.

Ramsey flinched. "And don't do that," he spat, gesturing toward the hand with which Jay had just crossed his heart.

Jay nodded wildly again.

Ramsey smiled, and it was almost charming, despite the fangs and glowing eyes. "Get a load of this." He turned, and in the space of two seconds melted and reformed into the shape of a wolf. The wolf made a chuffing sound deep in his throat and trotted away, disappearing into the gloom.

Later that night, Lizzy held Jay's jacket up to the light and wondered how it had gotten so dirty and why there were five ragged holes in the front of it. She went into his room to ask him about it and found him drawing another picture. It looked like a blond-haired devil with a charming smile.

"What are you drawing, honey?" she asked.

He turned in his chair to look at her, an expression of consideration drawing his eyebrows together. "I think it's another kind of angel."

"He looks awful mean," Lizzy said.

Jay turned back to his picture. "Don't you always say, 'Never judge a book by its cover'?"

Hero Sword

Rael's buckets were full of berries. They were nearly ripe, so they would keep for a while. Mara would be so happy to have something to brighten up their meals after the long winter. Last year, Kip had gotten into the early berries and eaten nearly half of a bucket full. Not only was he sick, but his mouth was dyed a reddish-blue color for the better part of a week. Rael hoped that his five-year-old son had not lost his taste for the tart, little treats.

The forest was alive with birdsong. Squirrels and chipmunks scampered from one limb to another. The buzz of insects droned in the trees, but the breeze on the path was strong enough to discourage most of them from pestering him. The sun was bright and warm. Rael felt wonderful.

The full buckets in his hands were little burden. His muscles were hard and ropey from years of labor. He made a good living from his farm, and his family always had enough to eat though they worked hard for it. The sun had already begun to redden his skin, which was fair and would never truly tan. By the end of the summer, his skin would be a red-gold color, the same color as his hair and close-cropped beard.

Rael was feeling so peaceful and relaxed that he initially failed to notice the movement of something large in the trees. When his eyes did move toward the sound, he expected to see nothing more frightening than a deer. Instead, he saw a Rogrum charging at him with a short, crude sword drawn. There was no war cry, only the rustle of dense underbrush. Its leering, simian face showed no evidence of humanity, only bloodlust.

Rael threw himself back from the attack and lost his footing. One of the heavy, ironbound buckets flew out from his flailing hand and struck the Rogrum a terrific blow on the side of the head. The nasty, jagged blade of the sword missed Rael's face by inches.

Rael got to his feet before the Rogrum did. He had no real training as a fighter and little experience aside from a few tavern brawls as a younger man. Some instinctive part of him, however, did not hesitate and lose his advantage. He grasped the handle of the other bucket, which was still close at hand, and brought it down on the creature's head with all of his might. Rael wasn't sure if the cracking sound came from the bucket or from the Rogrum's head, but he was sure that the Rogrum would not get up again.

He only had a moment to look at the dead creature at his feet before he heard more movement in the underbrush near the side of the path. Three more Rogrum were bearing down on him. He'd gotten lucky with one, but he had no chance against three. He ran.

Rael threw himself into the woods on the opposite side of the path. He was fit, and his long stride allowed him to widen the distance between himself and his bandy-legged pursuers. From what Rael had heard of the Rogrum, they were tireless and relentless. His mind would not calm down enough to think clearly. He was desperate, and he knew that if he didn't come up with a plan, he would likely die.

Rael caught a glimpse of darkness behind dense vines on the side of a low bank. In that moment, he made the decision to go to ground. He hoped he had enough of a lead to effectively hide himself. If not, he would go down fighting.

The darkness behind the vines was a small cave. The entrance was so low that he had to crawl on his belly to fit. He hoped that no animals made their den there, but he'd rather face an angry groundhog than three Rogrum. The heavy vines fell back into place after he'd squirmed into the dark recess. Less than thirty seconds later, he heard his pursuers pass.

The inside of the cave was small. He could not sit completely upright, and he could touch all sides of it by stretching out his legs. The smell of the place was earthy, and it felt cool and damp, but there was no sign of animal habitation. He found this a little strange because it seemed ideal for an animal dwelling.

The cave provided him with a reprieve, but he needed to decide what to do quickly. In the time of his own father's childhood, the Rogrum had invaded from the east in a massive, organized army. They'd come in dark wave after wave. They were broad-shouldered, slouching creatures with sloping foreheads and long matted hair, usually black or mud brown. Their skin was as white and lumpy as porridge, and it was mottled with irregular gray or brown spots and whorls.

The Rogrum were primitive, organized loosely by clans. Some wore coarsely woven cloth clothing, but equally as many wore the skins of animals. They knew basic metal working, but many of them still used flint tipped spears. The only time they had moved on a large scale, they were being led by a stranger to them, a tall straight man of some other race. His name was Krel-Nexa. Normally, they raided towns along the marches, but Rael's village was more than thirty miles from the border.

Rael gasped aloud. His village! Were the Rogrum headed for his village? What would they do to Mara and Kip? He nearly crawled out of his hiding space to run home immediately, but his reason grabbed hold. A headlong rush into the Rogrum would only get him killed. He said a short prayer to All-Father and lay back on the floor of the cave. Something hard and round was under his head. When he grabbed it to move it away, he found that it was attached to a larger object.

Feeling about in the darkness, he found that the round object was the pommel of a naked sword. He crawled to the mouth of the cave, so he could see it in the light. He expected it to be eaten with rust, or if it was bronze, caked with green deposits. It was, however, sound. The sword was plain. There was no ornamentation. The blade was straight, double-edged, and sharp. The crosspiece was functional, the grip wrapped in strips of brown leather, and the pommel a simple sphere. The overall length of the weapon looked about three feet.

Rael spoke aloud, "Is this a sign All-Father? I am no warrior. I only want to protect my family, my village. Please, help me."

Rael felt the hairs on his arms rise. He felt a static charge in the air as though a great storm were coming. Suddenly, his mind was pulled open, and an overwhelming flood of images, thoughts, and emotions poured into him. His body went rigid with them. He felt like his head would burst.

Then, it was over. His entire body throbbed with his heartbeat, and his head felt like it was made of waterlogged wood. But his mind was singing. The chaos that filled it was settling. He was able to make sense of it. What had just happened to him was amazing and overwhelming, but now, he understood.

This sword was Laoch-Meabhair. It had been carried by eighteen men. All of their accumulated knowledge and skill was somehow stored in the weapon. Each new technique and insight into opponents learned by each wielder over nearly a millennium was now Rael's. Four of those eighteen wielders had extensive experience fighting the Rogrum.

Rael crawled out of the cave. He looked around to get his bearings, and he saw that the Rogrum had doubled back and had spotted him. The three of them loped toward him confident that they could defeat him if he stood his ground or run him down if he fled.

Rael felt calm, balanced, and confident. The knowledge he'd gained was not just in his mind; it was in his body. That knowledge flowed easily through several lifetimes of practice and application. The sword itself thrummed in his hand. He knew Laoch-Meabhair would always be sharp and sound: no normal force could destroy it.

The center Rogrum charged him directly, and the other two flanked him as he expected. Rael did not wait; he charged. The creatures were stunned and hesitated for only a moment. They were used to certain reactions, and rarely had any of them seen an overmatched opponent rush to his death. Rael changed direction five strides from the center Rogrum. He darted toward the left Rogrum.

The startled creature swung his crude sword clumsily while also trying to avoid the brunt of Rael's rush. Rael danced past the squat creature. The blade flickered, and the Rogrum collapsed grasping his ankle and crying out gutturally.

The other two Rogrum skidded as they reversed direction. They approached more warily this time. One of them carried a sword. The other carried a short spear and wore a long knife on a thong tied about his middle. Having seen Rael's speed and precision, neither seemed willing to make the first move.

Long moments stretched out. Rael was balanced on the balls of his feet but still managed to affect an air of calm patience. He noticed the Rogrum darting glances at each other. Their companion still rolled around on the ground behind them groaning and holding his bloody ankle.

Finally, the spear carrier hurled his weapon. Rael moved like flowing water, and the spear passed harmlessly to clatter against a tree. When the Rogrum saw that his play had failed, he simply turned and ran.

His companion looked in surprise at his unexpected flight, and Rael ran him through. The creature was dead with its heart pierced before it hit the ground.

Rael did not chase the fleeing Rogrum, nor did he dispatch the injured one. He immediately ran toward his village. His stride was long and loping, designed to eat ground but not wind him. He knew he'd need to fight and was already running scenarios through his mind.

Rael saw few signs of the Rogrum on the hard-packed dirt of the road, but as he neared his village, he heard the bell in the square clanging wildly. When he got closer, he heard the clash of weapons and cries of fear, pain, and rage.

The part of Rael's mind that was strictly his own was frantic with worry for his family. The accumulated wisdom and experience from all of the recent additions to his mind kept him calm and focused. He kept his pace and breathed regularly. When he reached the edge of the last cluster of trees before the village clearing, he paused to observe.

He saw relatively few Rogrum. They were a raiding party after all, maybe thirty in number. The bulk of the fighting seemed to be taking place in the town square. A knot of men, armed mostly with farm tools were led by Jax, a retired soldier. There were maybe a dozen villagers against twenty Rogrum. He could see others darting from building to building looting. If the men in the fields heard the bell, they would arrive soon, but the men in the square would not last long.

Rael moved quickly and quietly toward the back of the Rogrum band. Some of the warriors in his head had codes of ethics that forbade them from attacking an opponent from the rear, but they were far outnumbered by the pragmatists. And Rael understood that he made all of the decisions, and he would do what needed to be done to protect his family and community.

The first three Rogrum fell before they knew they were under attack. Rael only went for a kill if it was convenient. His first priority was to incapacitate as many as possible. There were scattered cheers from villagers when they saw Rael so effectively join the fray.

For a moment, the Rogrums' obvious dismay made Rael think that they might flee, but then he saw their hideous, animal faces split into evil grins. Then, they turned their backs on him and threw themselves at the villagers again. Rael felt the urge to hack them to pieces from behind, but the accumulated wisdom of Laoch-Meabhair screamed at him to dive.

Rael dived and felt and heard a blade whistle through the air where he had just been. He rolled on his shoulder and came up facing the opposite direction. He barely had time to get his sword up to block a jarring blow from a tall, fierce-looking warrior. He was definitely not a Rogrum. His features were fine, and his skin was swarthy. His armor and sword were finely wrought. And Rael recognized him, or rather Laoch-Meabhair did.

It was Krel-Nexa, the man who had led the Rogrum fifty years earlier. This man, however, looked young, no more than thirty. He looked just as he did when Laoch-Meabhair's last wielder had seen him on the battlefield.

This recognition took place in a fraction of a second because that was all the time Rael had before having to defend against Krel-Nexa's powerful and blindingly fast onslaught. Rael was only able to move defensively. There was no opportunity to attack, and Rael found himself losing ground.

Rael noticed something that gave him heart, though. Krel-Nexa's expression showed doubt, even fear. He had no doubt believed that no one could stand against him, yet a farmer was now holding his own. Rael was more grateful than ever for the strength and stamina he had gained through hard work in his fields, but this intense fighting was a physical effort unlike any he had experienced before. Fear began to creep into his own thoughts, but the eighteen veterans who had become a part of him kept him parrying and looking for an opening.

Before the opportunity came, however, Krel-Nexa's blade slipped through Rael's guard and glanced painfully across his ribs. The veterans in his mind had been injured often and assessed the injury as minor and kept up the fight. Krel-Nexa was nonplussed when he got no reaction from Rael and let his own guard down for the smallest of moments. It was enough. Rael drove the tip of his own blade into the gap between Krel-Nexa's left shoulder plate and his breast plate. The chain link underneath took much of the power of the blow, but Rael felt two inches of the blade scrape through.

Rael barely had time to wrench the sword free and avoid Krel-Nexa's counterthrust. Rael lost his balance and staggered backward. Already, the veterans were taking his backward momentum and using it for a reverse roll which brought Rael back up into a kneeling position.

Krel-Nexa looked both astonished and frustrated at Rael's skill. In that moment, Rael saw or sensed something about his opponent. He wasn't human. His timeless appearance and his incredible ability with a sword only added to this intuitive belief. Knowing what Krel-Nexa actually was was another matter entirely.

The two swordsmen faced each other. Rael was discouraged to observe that Krel-Nexa didn't even appear to be winded. Rael may have been in excellent physical condition, but he had his limits. His veteran experience gave him ways to compensate for his growing fatigue, but he would eventually fall.

The two swordsmen waded in again. Krel-Nexa's assault was relentless. Rael danced, thrust, and parried, but Krel-Nexa's sword point repeatedly nipped at Rael's un-armored body. Twice Rael slipped on weakening legs, and twice he recovered in time, but he felt doomed to fall.

Then, he heard a cheer. He would not take his eyes from his opponent, but Rael knew that the men had arrived from the fields armed with their hoes and pitchforks. In his peripheral vision, he saw the fleeing shapes of Rogrum. Krel-Nexa's eyes darted toward his retreating soldiers for a fraction of a second, and Rael thrust Laoch-Meabhair with all of his waning might into Krel-Nexa's stomach.

Krel-Nexa lashed out, and Rael lost his grip on his sword. Krel-Nexa's injury was severe. He yanked Laoch-Meabhair free, tossed it away, and turned to run. He obviously didn't expect Rael to pursue because he did nothing to avoid the tackle that brought him to his knees. Rael was a big man, but even injured as he was, Krel-Nexa was able to throw him off.

Rael was just beginning to climb to his shaking feet again when he saw Jax leap through the air and collide with Krel-Nexa. Krel-Nexa was overpowering the burly old warrior when another villager and another leaped on him as well. Blades flashed as they rose and fell on Krel-Nexa.

With Laoch-Meabhair in hand, Rael ran and staggered and ran toward his own modest cottage on the outskirts of the village. The door was open and sagging on its hinges. He felt as though a fist squeezed his heart. He called out when he was twenty yards from the door, and he heard Mara answer, "I'm here!"

He felt his tension release at the sound of her voice.

He stepped across the threshold and nearly tripped over the dead Rogrum sprawled on his living room floor. Mara sat with Kip at their kitchen table. Her blouse was torn, but she looked unharmed. A bloody cleaver lay close at hand on the tabletop. She smiled and held out her arms. He lifted her up and held her in his arms. He felt Kip's small arms wrap around his waist. He stooped to lift the boy, and Mara and Rael held the child between them.

Later, but before nightfall, Rael had the body of Krel-Nexa burned along with the dead Rogrum. The villagers looked at Rael with a certain awe and followed his instructions to the letter. They hesitated, but only for a moment, when he told the blacksmith to melt down the fine sword and armor Krel-Nexa had worn. It seemed a waste, but Rael knew that Krel-Nexa had supposedly been killed in battle fifty years earlier, yet he had survived to attack Rael's own common, farming village. Caution regarding Krel-Nexa was something that each of the veterans in Rael's mind agreed upon.

He told everyone who wanted to listen about finding the sword, but he didn't tell them about having the memories and skills of eighteen seasoned warriors at his disposal. Everyone agreed that the sword was a blessing from All-Father, and they believed it was special. Anyone who saw Rael use it would have to believe that. Rael had always been well-liked, but that day, he became a hero.

Despite the eighteen veterans, Rael remained Rael. There was no vying for control or altering of his personality. He didn't think that the veterans' souls were kept in the sword, only a record of what they had learned and accomplished. He felt proud to be a part of it.

Rael told Mara everything. He always did. They not only discussed the blessing of Laoch-Meabhair, but also the responsibility of it. Such a wonderful gift would be wasted in the uneventful life of a farmer. How best could the sword be used? Did they want to give up their pleasant, comfortable existence? Could Laoch-Meabhair be passed to someone new?

They agreed to finish out the season. After the autumn harvest, they would decide what to do.

Empath

Andrew Dann looked down at the body of the dead girl lying on the threadbare, green carpet. He felt the sadness and disgust he always felt at the pointless death of a young person who had barely lived. His job as a homicide detective was generally unpleasant, but for Dann it was more unpleasant than it was for most. His gift made him good at his job, but that same gift often showed him the worst of human nature.

Dann stepped away from the girl. He watched the forensic technicians gather fibers, dust for prints, photograph ligature marks, and perform any other number of tasks which may or may not provide anything useful. The science was amazing, but it had limits. He would look more closely at the photos later on, but forensic evidence was not where his strength lay.

Jimmie Kent came to stand next to Dann. They both watched the technicians at work. Kent was ten years younger than Dann. He had just made detective at the age of thirty-one, and he was eager to learn everything Dann had to teach him.

Kent was an athletic, sandy-haired man whose biceps strained against the fabric of his short-sleeved shirt. He was a man who was sure to get in at least three visits to the gym every week and played intramural soccer in the spring and basketball in the winter. There was a healthy wholesomeness about Kent that made him look like he had stepped out of a Norman Rockwell print. Dann liked him well and thought he would go far.

"What do you think?" Kent asked. "Is the Andy Dann magic brewing?"

"Interviews and interrogations are my strong suits," Dann said. "We'll get to that soon enough."

People thought that Detective Andrew Dann was very intuitive, but they weren't even half right. Dann couldn't read minds, but he could read people. He actually had to work to shut them out. After forty years of practicing, he was good at it, but when he was tired or anxious, his defenses weakened. He knew what people were feeling. In truth, he actually felt what other people were feeling. It could be overwhelming. He had gotten a handle on his condition, but it was something he actively had to manage.

Dann began to dial down his defenses, and he felt Kent's intense curiosity and his pity toward the dead girl. The lab technicians were finishing up. One was feeling impatient and a little anxious. Dann guessed that he had a hot date planned. One was excited about being so close to violent death. Another older tech was just bored.

Dann was just about to suggest to Kent that they begin interviewing the people who lived in the other apartments in the building, but he felt a hot lance of fear pierce his chest, someone else's fear. He spun on his heel to take in all of the people in the room. He saw no one displaying signs of anxiety, but he heard quick steps in the hallway.

Dann took off at a dead run. He was into early middle age, but he was fit and fast. He just caught a glimpse of someone darting down the stairs. Kent was at his heels. The two detectives leaped down entire flights at a time and were almost upon a small, dark man as he crashed into the door at the foot of the stairs. Unfortunately for the dark man, the door opened inward.

He clumsily scrabbled at the door, but he didn't seem able to work the simple mechanism in his panicked state. The detectives each grabbed one of the man's arms and turned him around.

Dann was able to wrestle the little man's wild panic down to manageable levels in his own chest. The wall Dann constructed was porous, though. He was aware of the man's emotions, but he was protected from the force of them.

The little man's small black eyes stopped jittering, and Dann could feel his panic slowly give way to the resignation to capture. Then, the resignation turned to a calm, confident cunning. Dann guessed that the man believed himself to be a good enough liar to get out of his predicament.

"Where were you going in such a hurry?" Kent asked casually.

"I'm late for church," the man said.

"The preacher will forgive you when he learns that you've been helping the police solve a horrible crime," said Kent. The detective gave the little man a nudge back toward the stairs. "This way."

Dann went up the stairs first. The man followed, and Kent brought up the rear. At the top of the stairs, Dann asked the man's name. It was Antonio Rambaldi.

Dann took a clipboard from a uniformed officer who was posted in the hall. He looked over the papers there. He looked at Rambaldi and asked, "What were you doing on the fourth floor? Your apartment is on the second."

Rambaldi said, "I like to get my exercise. Why go to the gym and walk up fake stairs when I got real stairs here?"

"Were you coming up to see Molly Shea?" Dann asked.

Nothing changed on Rambaldi's face. He was a good liar, but Dann felt the stab of fear that the little man felt at the mention of the dead girl.

"Is she that little redhead that wears too much eye makeup?" Rimbaldi asked.

"Let's go see her." Dann said.

There was another jab of fear, but Rambaldi only shrugged his shoulders. "Anything to help the boys in blue."

Dann didn't get a chance to take Rambaldi into Shea's apartment before two men from the medical examiner's office carried the girl out on a stretcher. The three policemen and Rambaldi stood aside to let the men maneuver past them in the narrow hallway.

Rambaldi still looked calm, but Dann felt such strong shock from him that he was sure in a moment that the little man did not kill the girl. There was something between the two, though. There was a reason that Rambaldi bolted and a reason for his fear of capture.

Dann, Kent, and Rambaldi entered Molly Shea's apartment. They walked into the living room. Rambaldi's calm exterior remained intact, but Dann felt the internal flinch and disgust the little man felt when he saw the white outline which marked where Shea had recently been lying. It seemed that Rambaldi had felt some measure of affection for the girl.

Dann decided to take a shot in the dark. "She was a little young for you wasn't she, Rambaldi."

Rambaldi smirked. "Get your mind out of the gutter, copper."

Dann felt him relax. Rambaldi thought he knew where the questioning would go, and he felt confident. There had been no affair.

Dann decided to take another shot in the dark. "It must have been about the drugs, then."

Rambaldi's fright actually showed on his face and in his posture. It was like a splash of ice water in Dann's face. Bull's eye.

Kent had picked up on Rambaldi's reaction, and he tensed in case the man tried to make a break for it.

Dann said, "Antonio, we're from homicide, not vice. We don't care about your business unless it pertains to Molly Shea's death." He paused. "If you give us something useful, we'll let you go."

Rambaldi relaxed slightly, and Dann thought he would play ball. Dann sometimes wondered if he could project his emotions as well as pick up the emotions of others because he was usually able to put people at ease if he wanted to do so.

Rambaldi sat down heavily on the ratty, gray couch which had until recently been Molly's. He sighed heavily. Dann felt resignation in the man again.

"Molly carries merchandise for me. Every month or so she takes. . . took a small, black gym bag to the bus station and put it in a locker. Another party would pick it up in a day or two. She didn't cost much. It was worth the money to keep attention off me."

Dann nodded to Kent and said, "Check with the uniform in the hall."

After Kent went out, Dann said, "You liked her."

Rambaldi sighed again. "She was a good kid." He took a picture of her from an end table. In it she was smiling broadly. Her cheeks were rosy, and the green, paisley scarf she wore brought out the bright color of her eyes. "I don't know why she had anything to do with that punk."

"What punk?" Dann asked.

Before Rambaldi could respond, Kent came back into the room. "No black gym bag was logged by the evidence team. I think they would have noticed a bag full of drugs."

Dann's eyes never left Rambaldi. Dann asked again, "What punk?"

Rambaldi looked from Dann to Kent to Dann again. He smiled wryly. "The hophead."

The hophead was Billy Brooks. Apparently, he and Shea had had a volatile, on-and-off relationship. Molly Shea was trying to straighten out her life, and Billy was the kind of guy to discourage her just so he would have company on his downward spiral.

Kent called in for Billy Brooks's last known address, and the detectives headed there in an unmarked cruiser. Billy lived with this mother in another part of town just as rundown and depressed as the one they were leaving. The drive was short.

Dann and Kent were let inside the front door by the building super. He was a fat, greasy man who needed a shave, but he genuinely wanted to help the police. He said that he hadn't seen Billy that day, but he saw him often. Of course, he had been in the basement setting rat traps, and Billy might have come in then.

Kent knocked on the second-floor apartment where Billy and his mother lived. The door opened a few inches, and the detectives could see that it was secured by a chain. From inside peered the surprisingly pretty face of a middle-aged woman.

The woman looked at the detectives blankly, but Dann could feel her anxiety. It simmered just below the surface. She knew who they were, and she feared them.

"We're police m'am," said Kent, and he flashed his badge along with his wholesome, handsome smile. "May we come in to ask you some questions?"

Dann felt her anxiety leap a couple of notches. He thought that Billy was inside, but he had no probable cause for breaking down the door. It'll only take a couple of minutes," Dann said and tried to project goodwill. Her tension remained high.

Dann let down his defenses more and began to get vague, emotional impressions of other people in the building. Another person in the apartment was shining like a lighthouse of fear, however. The woman at the door was playing it cool. There was no reason for them to force their way in.

Then, almost impulsively, Dann shouted, "Halt! Police!"

Inside the apartment, the already high anxiety signature spiked. Something crashed inside the apartment. The startled woman yelped. Something else crashed.

Dann turned to Kent and said, "He's running."

Kent dashed for the stairs. Dann doubted if he would get down quickly enough to catch the fleeing suspect, so he stayed. He turned to the partially opened door and growled in his most intimidating voice, "You're going to let me in or I'm going to knock down that door."

When Kent returned, he was breathing heavily. Dann was inside the apartment staring down at the woman. She was sitting on a small upholstered chair. Her pretty face was set in stubborn lines.

Dann looked up. "Kent, this is Mrs. Evelyn Brooks. She's Billy's mother." His eyes went back to the woman. "Where did he go?" Dann asked.

Evelyn glared, her mouth a tight, straight line. She projected nothing but defiance.

Finally, she said in a tight voice, "You had no right to break in here."

Dann said, "I heard a crash and a scream."

Kent added, "It's true. Plus, you opened the door. It's not broken."

Evelyn growled, "He threatened to break it down."

Kent said, "Huh, I guess I didn't hear that part."

"If you tell us where he went, things will go easier for him," Dann said in a reasonable voice.

"I'm not saying a word," she said with a sneer.

Dann turned to Kent. "Billy has a sheet, right?"

"Yep."

"Call in for known associates and have a couple of uniforms sent over, please," said Dann.

Kent left the room.

Dann paced around the room, and Evelyn sat and looked gloomy. Just as Kent entered the room, Dann felt a jab of fear from Evelyn. His eyes leaped instantly to the woman. Her eyes were on the floor, but she was afraid of something. Dann thought that she'd seen something, but he hadn't looked quickly enough to see where she had been looking.

Dann began walking around the room again. It was like a game of hot and cold. When he walked toward her, her fear lessened, but when he walked back toward the door to her bedroom, the fear increased. In her bedroom was a broken window that opened onto a fire escape. That accounted for one of the crashes they had heard. The other was caused by a lamp that had been pulled from a dresser when someone tripped on the cord. Blood on the windowsill suggested that someone may have put a hand through the glass when he tripped on the lamp cord.

Evelyn had seen something in the living room, though, which had caused her anxiety. It was something near the door. His eyes roamed. Kent waited patiently, knowing that something was going on. Then, Dann saw it, a green, paisley scarf.

"Hey, Kent, do you have an evidence bag?" he asked.

"Yep," he said. He snapped on a latex glove and pulled a ziplock bag from an inner pocket. He followed Dann's eyes. "Is that Molly Shea's scarf?" he asked.

"It certainly looks like it," said Dann. It looks like it's taken some abuse too, like it was maybe used to strangle a girl."

Behind them, they heard a mouse-like squeak. Evelyn was staring wide-eyed at the little piece of green satin. Sharp regret radiated from her. She had been careless. She had not covered her son's trail. She slumped onto the chair and buried her face in her hands. Her shoulders shook with silent emotion.

Dann stood next to Evelyn. He felt no sympathy for her, but he put gentleness into his voice and tried to project compassion. "They'll go easier on him at the DA's office if you help us out."

"You don't care about my boy," she said in a strangled voice. Her tear-stained face was hard with stubbornness. "I won't do anything to help you."

"Do you know where he went?" Dann asked.

Her face remained hard and unresponsive, but he felt a tightening of her resolve. Dann thought she knew, but she would never tell.

Dann turned to Kent. "Hey, Jimmy, do you have that list of known associates?"

Evelyn tensed emotionally. Dann smiled slightly. Kent could see the smile, but Evelyn could not. Kent smiled in return. Here was the Dann magic.

Kent took out a small notebook with a leather cover and flipped it open. He opened his mouth to begin reading the names aloud, but Dann motioned for him to hand it over. He wanted to be able to read at his own pace, to linger here or there. He might even want to repeat names or asked questions. She wouldn't answer, but he would know.

"Evelyn." Dann said the name intimately as though they were friends. "Would Billy have gone to see his cousin, Steve?"

She sat stubbornly silent, and she gave no emotional indicator.

"How about Russell, his cell mate from his last stretch?" Dann asked casually.

Again, there was no response from Evelyn.

"Billy was busted with a girlfriend for possession two years ago."

Evelyn remained stone-faced, but she flinched inwardly.

"Her name was Kristen, I believe," said Dann. "Kristen Meyer."

Inwardly, Evelyn was squirming, but she was putting forth a mighty effort to give nothing away.

"Do we have a current address for Kristen Meyer?" Dann asked.

"I bet we do," Kent said.

Dann smiled at Evelyn. "Why don't we send a cruiser over there to check her out."

Inside Evelyn was screaming. Her external facade was cracking too. When she reached up to brush a lock of hair from her forehead, he saw a slight tremor in her hand.

Dann left Kent in the room with Evelyn and went to the hall to talk to a uniformed officer. "Take Mrs. Brooks to the station for questioning. Don't let her use the phone for an hour or so. I don't want her calling Billy to warn him."

The officer went into the apartment, and moments later, he left with Evelyn. Kent followed them out. He stopped next to Dann. "What's next?"

Dann said, "We're going to call in for a couple more officers to back us up, and then, we're going to Kristen Meyer's house."

The drive to Meyer's house was short, only a few blocks. The neighborhood was nearly as run down, but the Meyer residence was an actual house and not an apartment building. There was junk in the back yard, old washing machines and car parts. It looked as though some effort was taken to keep the front yard mowed, however, and the paint on the house looked fairly new.

"What's the plan?" Kent asked from the driver's seat of the unmarked police cruiser. "I don't think we have probable cause to get a warrant for Meyer's place. Are we just going to stake it out.?"

Dann smiled. "We didn't initially have probable cause to enter the Brooks apartment, but that worked out for us."

"Magic?" Kent asked.

"Presto! Watch me produce a murderer from this ordinary house."
Dann opened the car door and walked over to the patrol car which was
just driving up. He asked the officers to cover the back of the house, and
he and Kent approached the front door.

Dann mentally braced himself and lowered his emotion defenses.
He felt the nervous excitement rolling from Kent. As he neared the
house, he also began to feel emotional signatures from two people inside
the house. One of them was curious. The other was terrified. Dann
wondered if Kristen Meyer knew anything about her friend's activities
earlier that afternoon.

Kent stood beside the door. His gun was drawn, but it was held
low beside his leg. Dann knocked on the door and stood slightly to the
other side. As they waited for a response, Dann felt the curious person
become wary. Dann guessed that Billy was telling Kristen to tell the
police that he wasn't there.

The door opened and a pretty, dark-haired girl stood on the other
side of the closed screen door. She was pale and too skinny, but she had
an art-student appeal. She wore faded jeans and a white T shirt with a
Kermit the Frog decal.

"May I help you?" she asked.

Dann held out his badge for her inspection. "We're police. Have you seen Billy Brooks today?"

Dann could tell that she expected this. She cocked her hips to one side and said, "I haven't seen him." She seemed nonchalant, but Dann could feel curiosity.

Dann said, "We're with homicide, Miss."

Her mouth fell open. Dann didn't need to be empathic to sense her shock. It was all over her face.

"What. . . he wouldn't." She was unable to form words for a moment. Dann could feel her center herself, but she was an emotional girl by nature. She tried to appear the faithful friend, but she was full of doubt and turmoil. It seemed that she believed Billy capable of murder.

"We believe he killed a girl named Molly Shea earlier today," Dann said.

Kristen's mouth dropped open again, and her eyes widened. In a quiet, little-girl voice, she said, "Molly?"

"Yes, she was strangled," said Dann. He could feel how shaken the girl was. He guessed that they had been friends. Dann added, "Billy absconded with a black gym bag containing drugs."

Kristen looked intently into Dann's eyes. Her jaw firmed, and her mouth drew into a tight line. The loss she felt did not vanish, but anger grew and transformed her emotions into something else. . . resolve.

She opened the screen door and stepped out onto the porch. She held the door for the detectives and said, "Billy is inside. He has a bag like you described."

As the men began to walk past her into the house she added, "Be careful. Billy sometimes carries a little black gun in his pocket."

Kent stopped, turned, and jogged out to the side yard. He put his fingers into his mouth and whistled loudly. He motioned to the officers behind the house so that they would be on their guard. He then jogged back up to the porch with his gun drawn. Dann took his own gun out of the holster under his arm, and the detectives entered.

Dann made a show of moving from room to room with Kent and making sure it was clear before moving on. He knew where Billy was, however. He could feel Billy's desperate fear throbbing like a rotten tooth. When the detectives reached the hall closet where Billy hid, Dann motioned Kent to take up position to one side, and Dann took up position on the side with the knob.

He grabbed the knob, twisted it, and threw the door open, but he did not move to look inside. Three hard, sharp pops sounded from the closet, and drywall powder puffed out from the three holes which seemed to magically appear on the wall opposite. Silence followed.

Dann could feel Billy's indecision. Billy was a cornered rat: he would bite, but it was not on his nature to go on the offensive. He was working himself up to action. There was an emotional "click" when Billy was galvanized into action. Dann knew it as soon as Billy did, and he brought the barrel of his .38 down as hard as he could onto the wrist of Billy's gun hand as soon as it emerged from the closet. Bones broke with a pop not unlike the reports from Billy's gun, and he screamed in pain. The gun flew from Billy's hand and rebounded from the wall. Dann kicked it away.

Kent was not as gentle as he might have been when he handcuffed Billy's injured wrist. The gym bag and Billy's little .22 were taken as evidence. Kristen spat at Billy as one of the uniformed officers led him past her, and she said that she would be happy to make a statement and even testify against Billy in court.

Both Kent and Dann attended Molly's funeral. Many people were there. They saw Kristen and Antonio. Dann kept his shields firmly in place, but he saw the grief on the people's faces and thought it looked genuine. This made Molly's death seem both better and worse. Molly would be missed because she had obviously touched lives: better and worse.

Rusty Spur

The stranger walked into the Rusty Spur just as the sun began to color the horizon pink. His clothes were good but had seen much wear, and they were still covered with dirt from the trail. His flat-brimmed, low-crowned hat was pulled down just above his eyebrows, and two no-nonsense blue .44s rode low on his hips.

He walked slowly but with purpose across the saloon to the bar. I expected him to order a whiskey, as most people did, but he asked for a tall glass of water as well. He didn't sit but stood at an angle so that his back was mostly toward the bar and his face toward the door.

I'd only been working at the Rusty Spur for a couple of months. I'd originally come west to be a schoolteacher, but when I'd arrived at the town which had agreed to hire me, I found that it had ceased to exist. For the most part, anyway. The silver mine, on which the town's economy was based, dried up. I didn't have the money to return to Albany.

I found this town. It had both silver and cattle. Unfortunately, it also had more than enough schoolteachers. Well, a man has got to work, so I ended up here. I'd tended bar before, but Albany was nothing like this place.

There wasn't much of a crowd at that time of the day. The place really didn't start hopping until after dark, so I had some slow time in which to gather my resources, both literal and figurative. The bar was fully stocked, so the literal was taken care of. Sometimes, I kept a dime novel behind the bar, but the boss got annoyed when he saw me reading, but there was only so much a guy could wipe a clean bar.

I'm no gunfighter, but I know how to use a gun. I keep a Colt .38 behind the bar. I wouldn't take it out unless death were looking me in the eye. As I said, I'm no gunfighter.

The man who sipped the whiskey and the water in front of me was. A gunfighter, I mean. It was written all over him. He wasn't scared or anxious, but he was poised like a cat. He stared at the door like a tom watches a mouse hole. I couldn't help but to feel nervous.

I typically didn't talk to the clientele around the Spur unless they spoke to me first. They tended to be easily offended. If the gunfighter in front of me had had a tail, it would have been twitching back and forth. A "high-strung tension in repose" is how I would have described it, even if it was paradoxical.

"Where do you hail from?" I asked the gunfighter with a slight quiver in my voice. I didn't realize I was going to say anything until I did. Then, I feared he would plug me with one of those .44s.

He surprised me with a smile. His eyes never left the door, but his expression showed pleasant amusement. "I'm not from around here," he said. I'm not quite sure why he found that funny, but I was too happy about not having a slug between my eyes to give it much thought.

I tried my best to ignore the man, but he remained in my thoughts. My eyes kept jumping furtively from whatever I was doing then to the door. Something was going to happen, and I didn't want to be caught by surprise.

I heard the stranger sigh. I couldn't help but to look over at him. He had a pocket watch held at arm's length and up high. At first, I thought it was because he couldn't see well up close, but then I realized he just didn't want to take his eyes off the door.

He wasn't fidgety *per se*, but I could sense a mild agitation about him. Impatience radiated from him, but he wasn't surly or unpleasant.

I practically jumped out of my skin when he spoke to me all on his own.

"You see a pasty guy come in here lately?" he asked in a casual, just-passing-the-time drawl.

I have to admit that I stammered a bit. I felt so startled that I didn't even really understand what he said. I must have sounded like an idiot. "Uh. . . pasty guy?"

"Yeah, white as a fish belly." He paused. His eyes squinted as though he were trying to visualize the man in question, but they never left the doorway. "He's skinny too. Eyes black like tar. His hair is long and a bit frilly like a lady's."

I knew the guy he talked about. I didn't say so because I liked the guy, and I guessed the gunfighter wasn't his long-lost friend.

The fellow was some sort of aristocrat from Europe. He dressed neatly and expensively, and he always tipped well.

The gunfighter sensed my hesitation, and his eyes flicked toward me for a fraction of a second. He nodded as though that was all the answer he needed.

More people were arriving as the evening progressed, and soon I hadn't a spare moment to take watching that strange and dangerous man. I couldn't help but to wonder why he was interested in Renault. That was the European's name. I liked him quite a bit but not enough to take a bullet for him. I guess, even though I did my job the same as ever, I was interested to see how things played out.

The place got pretty raucous. Sid came in to play the piano, and some of the girls came from upstairs to do a couple of dance numbers. The patrons were slugging whiskey and beer like it was water. I wouldn't say that I forgot the stranger or stopped worrying about Renault, but they moved to the rear of my thoughts.

Someone shouted on the other side of the bar. I turned to the ruckus and saw a mountain of a man named Hank Roy, red-faced and shouting at the gunfighter. The gunfighter seemed indifferent to Hank except that Hank blocked his view of the door.

The gunfighter stepped to the side so he could see the door.

Hank shouted, "Look at me when I'm talkin' to you!"

Rage flashed in the gunfighter's eyes for just a moment. Then, he looked amused.

The room had gone quiet. Hank was a regular scrapper, and people expected it from him. This looked like it might be interesting. Hank wasn't very bright. Everyone else could sense the danger in the gunfighter and left him alone. Hank was just too dumb and too used to winning.

Hank made a grab at the gunfighter. The gunfighter simply stepped back and slapped Hank's hand aside. His eyes flicked to the door every few seconds despite his interactions with Hank.

Renault walked into the saloon just as Hank was yanking his hand back from another of the gunfighter's stinging slaps. The gunfighter registered Renault's presence immediately. Hank saw the gunfighter going for his guns and lunged at him. Hank liked to beat people up, and to do that he'd need to keep the gunfighter from drawing.

I wouldn't have sworn to this next part in court. I don't think anyone else in the Spur would either. Even the eighty of us holding together on it would probably be called crazy. Renault wasn't human. In that one moment, no one doubted it.

Renault saw the gunfighter, who was twisting away from Hank and could not keep his eyes on Renault. He snarled the way I'd seen mountain lions snarl. His lips curled back, and his nose wrinkled. I'd never noticed before, but his canine teeth were long and pointed.

The snarling and the fangs were plenty scary, but I swear to God I saw his eyes flash too. They looked like the ends of cigarettes when they're being inhaled.

Renault looked mad. He stayed in the doorway for a moment like he was deciding what to do. I wanted him to leave more than anything.

The saloon was as quiet as a crypt. Even big, stupid Hank had stopped grabbing at the gunfighter to see what was going on. His bulk still blocked the gunfighter, though.

Renault turned to flee but only took two steps before screaming like a trapped animal and stumbling back inside. He was shielding his eyes as though he were in bright sunlight and lurching backward. He kept up his snarling.

Striding into the saloon came a man all dressed in black trail clothes and a priest's collar. In one hand, he held a wooden cross about two feet long with the center piece sharpened to a point.

The gunfighter slammed one of his guns against Hank's neck, and the big man dropped like a sack of flour. Renault turned at the sound and locked eyes with the gunfighter. The eyes were full of hate and rage.

The gunfighter leveled both .44s at Renault as Renault leaped twenty feet through the air toward the staircase leading to the girls' rooms. The guns blazed. The slugs caught Renault and spun him like a top. He fell short of the staircase and slammed against the wall.

That's not the first time I heard gunfire at the Rusty Spur, but that didn't make it any less deafening. Everyone stood frozen and silent except for the gunfighter and the priest. They rushed forward.

I couldn't believe what I was seeing when Renault leapt, spitting and cursing, from his place against the wall. He was obviously angry, but he looked frightened as well. He clawed at the bullet holes with taloned fingers.

The priest shouted, "They're blessed bullets!"

Renault charged. The gunfighter's guns roared and bucked in his hands. Each slug tore at Renault's chest, and though he winced in pain, he didn't stop coming. The gunfighter and Renault collided and fell in a tangle of flailing arms and legs.

The next thing I knew, the gunfighter flew through the air and crashed into the bar. People who had been standing as still as statues moved all at once. I should have, but I didn't. I'm not sure why, but I think it has something to do with my reason for writing this story.

The bullet holes in Renault had begun to smolder. He advanced on the priest who held his cross in front of him. Renault shielded his eyes and moved forward anyway. He bared his teeth in what might have been a snarl or a grimace of pain.

The gunfighter tried to lift himself but fell again. The priest looked frightened and unsure of himself. The saloon had emptied except for just a few, but no one was doing anything.

"Hey!" I shouted. I didn't think about dying. I just acted. Seeing what Renault really was offended me on some basic level. I was normally an even-tempered, levelheaded man, but I felt angry.

"Hey!" I shouted as loudly as I could. My hand fastened around the butt of my .38.

Renault's eyes found me and flashed that red-orange color. I saw the priest reversing the cross to use it as a weapon, and I fired.

Of my six bullets, two struck Renault. He didn't even flinch, but he sure looked mad. Right up until the priest shoved the sharp end of the cross through his back, he looked like he wanted to tear my head off.

Renault screamed and clawed at the wooden stake sticking out of him. In desperation, he slashed at the priest, but the priest threw himself backward. Ribbons of black cloth flew through the air like confetti.

The gunfighter had gotten up while my attention was on the fight, and he moved forward. He looked shaky but resolved. In his left hand, he held a .44. In the right he held a big, heavy, banana-shaped knife.

Renault lunged again at the priest who had nowhere to go. He grabbed the priest by the tatters of his shirt front and drew him toward his slavering, fanged mouth.

The priest shouted, "In the name of Christ, be gone!"

Renault flinched but wouldn't let go. By that time, though, the gunfighter had gotten right behind him. The strange knife flashed, and Renault's head hung by a shred. It flashed again and Renault's head hit the floor. The body took a few faltering steps, felt at its neck, and fell.

The corpse decayed before my eyes. The putrid smell of rot rose and passed quickly. The torso and limbs sank in upon themselves as moisture rose from the body like a fog. In short minutes, all that remained was a dried husk.

The priest stood with his hands on his knees breathing heavily. "He was a young one," he said in the quick, gasping way that breathless people speak.

The gunfighter stood with his hand on the back of a chair swaying slightly. Lines of blood ran from a wound above his hairline.

He looked up at me and said matter-of-factly, "Thanks for the help." It was stated in a way he might have thanked someone for helping him to push a wagon out of the mud.

That was the first time that I ever saw something supernatural and knew what I was seeing. Renault was a vampire. He'd been staying in town but going out at night to attack more isolated settlements. Vampires, I learned, could travel fast. He drank the blood of people in order to mimic life, but he had been dead for over forty years.

Vincent and Sean, the gunfighter and the priest, were professional hunters. They worked for people who knew about monsters, and now, I would too.

Purpose

Leland was rarely bored. The world was too full of wonder for that. He sometimes felt adrift, however, without direction. He had been wandering for some time now, searching for the next thing, the next stage in his long life.

The cicadas grew quieter as the sun sank toward the horizon. Cultivated fields were interspersed with stands of trees and an occasional farmhouse. At the most recent farmhouse, children and dogs stopped playing in the yard and watched him as he passed. The driver of an old, rattling farm truck craned his neck as he passed Leland and nearly drove into a ditch. Leland was clearly not from around there.

As the land sloped down an especially lonely stretch, Leland spotted a crossroad a short distance away. A man stood in the middle of the intersecting roads. The man had his back to Leland, and Leland walked lightly, so he was able to get quite close without the man being aware of him.

The man was tall. His shabby, gray suit was too big for his thin frame. A small-brimmed fedora perched on the back of his head, and his skin was the color of dark chocolate. There was a sense of hopelessness about the man, a doom.

Leland purposely scuffed loose gravel, and the man spun around and stared at him wide-eyed like a rabbit when it hears baying hounds.

"Are you him?" the man asked in a rasping whisper.

"Excuse me?" Leland asked. "I am only a traveler on the road."

The man gave Leland an appraising look. He relaxed only slightly, and his eyes narrowed.

Leland was about six feet tall and muscular in the way that swimmers and divers are muscular. His red-gold hair was slightly too short to pull into a ponytail, and his eyes were a vibrant green.

Like the man in the crossroad, Leland also wore a gray suit, but his was immaculate. It had a fine blue pinstripe and was sharply creased. His shoes were dusty from the road, but they were clearly expensive. On his head he wore a lightweight, gray homburg. A gold watch winked below the cuff of his left sleeve.

The man asked, "You ain't got no car?"

"Sadly, no," replied Leland.

"You look like a man who'd have a car," the man said, markedly looking Leland up and down.

Leland shrugged elegantly. He was intrigued and wanted to continue the conversation, so he asked, "Were you expecting someone?"

The man simply stared at Leland as though he were trying to look through him. He seemed to make a decision. He sighed and said, "I suppose not."

"Where are you headed?" Leland asked.

The man spread his arms wide to take in the immediate area. "I was headed here."

"It's getting dark," Leland observed. "Where will you sleep?"

The man said nothing and merely spread his arms again.

"Can you use some company?" Leland asked. "I have no other commitments."

"I suppose that might be nice," he said. "I have some food. It ain't much, but you're welcome to some."

Leland's eyebrows rose, and he smiled widely. "Hospitality!" he said brightly and, in that moment, seemed nearly angelic.

"I am Leland Geary, and it is a pleasure to make your acquaintance," he said, holding out his hand.

The man took his hand and shook firmly. "My name is Franklin Cole."

They found a stone fire ring about thirty feet from the road. While Leland gathered wood for a fire, Cole retrieved a battered suitcase and an equally battered guitar case from behind some bushes. They warmed two cans of beans near the fire. They sat on wide logs near the ring and ate in a relative silence.

Cole opened his guitar case and lifted a battered Harmony from it. He picked out a melancholy tune, and the old mail-order instrument sounded mellow and sweet. Leland listened appreciatively. He had heard blues music in his travels and liked it a great deal. It was simple, direct, and honest.

"Why would you seek out this place?" Leland asked.

Cole paused in his playing. He was still, clearly in an attitude of contemplation.

Leland began to wonder if he would respond.

Cole sighed and shook his head. "Have you ever heard of a man named Robert Johnson?"

Leland nodded. "Is this that crossroad?"

"I believe it is," said Cole. He gently placed his guitar in its case and brought out a pint bottle of rye from his jacket pocket. "I ain't got proper glasses, but I'll buy you a drink."

"Thank you," Leland said and reached for the bottle. The sweetish whiskey burned down his throat and blossomed in his belly. He passed the bottle back to Cole who drank also.

Leland asked Cole to play more music. Cole said that he would be delighted, but as he reached for the guitar, his eyes went vacant then squeezed shut. He pressed his palm against his right eye socket. He hunched his shoulders, and his whole body seemed to go rigid.

Leland reached for him and asked, "What is the matter?"

Cole didn't respond at first, but in a few seconds, his body slackened and he said in a tight whisper, "It'll pass."

Leland felt again the fey premonition of doom for Cole. Leland closed his eyes and extended his senses in order to examine the phenomenon more closely.

When Leland opened his eyes, Cole was looking at him with a beetled brow. "What was that?"

Leland said, "I should ask the same question."

Cole shook his head, brought out the rye again, and sipped at it. "I get spells is all. They pass."

"Have you been to a doctor?" Leland asked.

Cole snorted a laugh and, aside from a slight grayish tone to his skin, looked much better. He corked the whisky but didn't put it away.

"Doctors ain't for free," Cole said and reached into a different pocket of his jacket. He took out a battered leather billfold. Everything the man had seemed old and worn. He took out a small black and white photograph and handed it to Leland.

"That is my wife, Bethany," Cole said. "She's about due to have our first child. I haven't been able to find work of any kind let alone play music, which is what I really want to do."

Leland was astonished at the beauty of the woman in the photograph. Her hair was close cropped around a heart-shaped face. Her large, dark eyes were her dominant feature. Her upper lip was relatively thin, and her lower lip was full, which gave her mouth a fine-drawn but ripe look. Her nose was small and straight. Her complexion was as smooth and dark as her husband's. She wore a floral-print house dress, and though she looked too thin, as many people were in those hard times, her lines formed a pleasantly feminine hourglass.

"She is lovely," Leland said as he passed the picture back.

"I know she is," said Cole. "I don't deserve her, and it breaks my heart that I can't provide for her."

"You're desperate enough to sell your soul to the devil?" Leland asked. "Like Robert Johnson?"

Without hesitation, Cole said, "I am. I have got to take care of Beth and the baby." He uncapped the rye and took another drink. Leland drank again as well.

"You thought I was the devil," Leland stated simply.

"I still ain't made up my mind," said Cole. "A well-dressed white man shows up at this crossroad at dusk with no car. It ain't the natural way." He gestured at Leland from head to toe. "You could probably buy a car if you hocked your clothes and that watch."

Leland smiled. "It wouldn't be a very fine car."

Cole snorted a laugh again.

"How often do you have spells?" asked Leland.

Cole shrugged his shoulders. "Now and again."

"There might be something wrong which a doctor could fix," Leland said.

"Man, I ain't got money for a doctor!" Cole snapped, unable to hide his frustration and anxiety.

"I do," said Leland.

Cole looked at him hard. "Why would you help a stranger like me?"

"Why wouldn't I? It's in my power."

Cole continued to look hard at Leland. "The devil don't give nothin' for free," he said.

"I'm not the devil," said Leland. "To my knowledge, he doesn't exist though there are other beings who are probably just as bad."

Cole uncapped the rye again. There wasn't much left. He handed it to Leland and asked, "What are you then? You ain't natural."

Leland drank, being sure to leave a swallow for Cole. "No one is more natural than I. My people are old. The Irish called us Daoine Sidhe."

Cole's eyes narrowed, "What's that?"

Leland smiled and said, "The People Under the Hills. The Fair Folk. Fairies."

"Like givin' people donkey heads kinda fairies?" Cole asked.

Leland shrugged.

"What were you doing after I had my spell? You had your eyes closed, and I. . . felt something."

Leland shrugged again. "My people see more of the world than yours see. I was simply looking more intently."

"What did you see?"

Leland looked at Cole for some time before saying, "An augury of your death."

Cole sighed, and his head drooped. "Yeah, I figured as much."

"These things which I see or sense are not certain. Medicine is much more than it once was," Leland said.

"Mostly, I worry about Beth," Cole said, looking at the empty whiskey bottle in his hands. "I'm about done in," he said and stood up. He took off his jacket, rolled it up for a pillow, and lay down to sleep.

Leland sat and watched the fire. He heard Cole's breathing grow deeper and turn into quiet snoring. Leland extended his senses once again toward Cole. He found that Cole's illness was beyond his powers or the powers of modern medicine. Leland lay down on the opposite side of the fire and slept.

When Leland woke the next morning, Cole was dead. He looked down at the man for a long time. He thought of all of the years behind him and all of the years still ahead. He thought of a beautiful, young woman with mahogany skin. He thought of the innate musical nature of his own people. He made a decision.

In only a few minutes, Cole lay on the ground in Leland's expensive suit, and Leland wore Cole's shabby one. Leland knelt on one knee and placed his right hand on the grass. He closed his eyes. A low, pulsing thrum built in intensity and seemed to sink into the earth. The ground rippled and opened up. Franklin Cole sank into the ground, and the soil and grass closed over him.

Leland stood. He closed his eyes again. Light separated itself from the morning air and gathered around him. His red-gold hair grew shorter and darker. His milky skin darkened as well, and his muscular frame grew thinner until the suit hung loosely from him.

Leland took the wallet from his pocket and found identification which bore the address of Franklin Cole. He replaced them, picked up the old suitcase and the old guitar case, and walked down the road with a sense of purpose.

Willow-Wood Box

Phelan scrabbled desperately through the underbrush dragging the sacred willow-wood box along with him. His nostrils stung with acrid smoke, his arms and hands were crisscrossed with numerous tiny cuts, and his stained robe hung in tatters. In the distance, he could hear shouting and an occasional scream of pain.

His chest heaved from exertion and fear. He couldn't decide whether to go to ground or put as much distance between himself and the Romans as he could. He was sure that he would be killed if the soldiers spotted him, but he didn't know how far their search would extend.

He was only a novice druid with much studying left to do, but that would probably never happen now. The soldiers had cut down the elders. Glyn was the last of them. He had given the seven sacred objects to the novices and charged the young men to preserve them and hide them. Phelan had not seen Glyn killed. The burley druid was wounded but still fighting, but who could stand against Rome?

Phelan felt a stinging on his cheeks, and he realized that he was weeping, and the salt tears were running over cuts. The Romans had set the sacred grove on fire. The old oak at the center of the grove was hundreds of years old, and soon it would be gone. All of the accumulated knowledge of the druid elders had run out of them in a red torrent.

Phelan took a few moments to center himself, and he decided quickly what to do. The Romans were thorough. He felt sure that they would cover all of the surrounding area closely. He would fly and hope to get out of their immediate range before nightfall.

The box was awkward, but he managed to grip it firmly and carry it under one arm. When he had the time, he would try to rig some sort of strap to hold it in place. Until then, he would jog along with it under his arm. He planned to switch from one arm to the other as he began to tire.

Phelan was already exhausted and sore in every muscle. Each jogging stride seemed to jar his whole body, and the lip of the box dug into the fingers of the hand holding it. Just as he was considering going to ground again, he heard a horrible sound: horsemen. He made a move to leap from the path, but the urgent shouting he heard behind him robbed him of the hope of escaping unseen.

He did leave the path. He hoped that the surrounding vegetation would slow the riders. Unfortunately, the ground was relatively level, and the trees were widely spaced in this part of the forest. He cursed under his breath and increased his speed as much as he was able.

The muffled sound of hooves on the soft earth quickly drew nearer. Phelan did not understand the language of the Romans, but he could hear the eagerness of their shouts and knew that they anticipated some fun. He would have to fight.

Phelan had no weapon. He carried nothing but he willow-wood box. He felt that his legs or his lungs would give out at any moment, and he actually felt the horse's breath gusting against the back of his neck. With every bit of his desperate strength, he spun around swinging the box. It connected solidly with the horse's head. The animal veered wildly, and its shoulder struck Phelan a stunning blow. Phelan went sprawling.

The druid was unable to see what happened, but he heard a terrific crash. He shook his head and lifted his aching body into a sitting position. The rider lay still at the base of a tree. His helmet was dented deeply, and he didn't appear to be breathing. The horse lay on its side breathing heavily and raggedly. Phelan felt a moment of regret and pity for the animal, but that was cut short by the rumble of more horsemen.

Two horsemen shouted and charged. Again, no weapon was at hand, so Phelan took up the box. He saw one of the soldiers stand in his stirrups and let his spear fly. Phelan instinctively brought the box up to protect himself. The weapon was deflected, but a deep furrow was dug across the finely carved wood.

The other horseman rode by Phelan in a thunder of hooves and thrust with his spear. Phelan dove and rolled. He wrenched his arm painfully, and the willow-wood box flew from his hands. His first impulse was to leap after the precious box, and the soldier anticipated that and wheeled his horse in that direction.

Phelan, however, threw himself in the other direction. He scrabbled over the body of the still gasping horse and retrieved the spear of the fallen soldier. The soldier who had thrown his spear had a short, thrusting sword in his hand, but his intention was obviously to trample the druid under the hooves of his horse. Phelan knew he would never get the spear up in time, but he tried. The shaft of the spear was raised only two feet from the ground when Phelan abandoned his attack and jumped out of the way. The horse's front legs straddled the spear shaft mid-gallop, and the horse went down taking the rider with it.

The soldier landed hard, and the air whooshed from his lungs. He tried to stand, but he was dazed and couldn't get his wind back. The horse was up again and galloping away at top speed.

Phelan spun to see the last horseman bearing down on him again. The druid had little experience with weapons, but he took up the fallen spear and hurled it at the approaching rider just has the rider threw his own. Phelan felt a line of hot pain sear his ribs and inner biceps on his left side. His spear struck the rider in the throat just above his breastplate. The soldier looked surprised for a moment and dropped from his saddle.

Phelan didn't hesitate. He made a grab for the horse's bridal, but the horse veered away and ran. He saw that the remaining soldier had gotten to his feet, but he still looked disoriented. Phelan briefly considered attacking the soldier, but dazed or not, the man was a trained killer, and the druid did not want to press his luck.

He grabbed the willow-wood box and ran. He didn't know how long he had before the pursuit recommenced, but he guessed that the Romans would be earnest now in tracking him down.

Phelan eventually spied a small cave opening. He had no idea how big the space inside was, but he felt like he could go no farther. He had to stoop slightly when he entered. He had no source of light, so he could make out no details, but he had a sense of a considerable space. He hoped the cave did not house any aggressive animals, but he was willing to take a chance.

He sat, chest heaving and eyes glazed and unfocused. Phelan was unaware of the passage of time. His brain was numb, and his body ached. The gashes along his ribs and biceps were shallow, but they burned like narrow lines of fire. He knew that he needed to plan a strategy to improve his chance of surviving his ordeal, but he felt totally incapable of thinking in a reasonable, organized way.

The druid sat just inside the mouth of the cave where he had some light to see. He looked at the willow-wood box. The spear had actually gashed a hole in the lid. Gray fur with a pattern of darker guard hairs could be seen within. It looked like a wolf pelt. The willow box made sense now because, like the wolf, willow was associated with the moon.

Phelan's curiosity was aroused which was a pleasant surprise for his numb brain. He'd seen plenty of wolf pelts, and he wondered why this would be considered one of the most sacred possessions of the druids. Without realizing it, Phelan had opened the box.

The pelt really was fine, maybe the finest he had ever seen, but it was more than a pelt. It was a hooded cloak with the wolf head making up the hood. The proportions were all wrong, however. There was no way that a wolf could have gotten so big. The cloak was long enough for a tall man, but it was made from only one hide.

Phelan was so engrossed with his study of the wolf pelt that he nearly lost his life. A spear bounced off the stones only a hand's breadth from his face. It clattered to the ground. He leaped to his feet and took up both the pelt and the spear.

Four Roman horseman were dismounting and heading in his direction. Phelan thought of his great fortune in the earlier skirmish with Roman soldiers, and he believed that more luck was too much to hope for. The cave opening would ensure that only one could attack at a time, but they were trained to fight. He felt sure that he would perish, and he did not want to die.

The soldiers shouted and jeered at the terrified druid. Phelan gripped the pelt more tightly and felt strangely comforted by it. He thought of his slaughtered friends and the pointless destruction of the sacred trees, and he began to feel angry. He expected to feel impotent frustration at his inability to effectively defend himself or even. . . have retribution.

Phelan realized that he felt less frightened than he had. A feeling of strength seemed to crawl up his arm from the tightly griped pelt. If he was to die, the druid decided that he would die fighting, garbed in the sacred cloak. He dropped the spear so that he could use both hands to clasp the cloak's willow-wood hook and eye beneath his chin.

Phelan felt power thrum through his body. All soreness and weariness vanished. His body felt strong and limber. His sense of smell sharpened abruptly which would have overwhelmed him except that it felt completely natural. Suddenly, he no longer felt like prey. He felt like a predator.

The soldiers froze. Their mouths dropped open in surprise. Then, their expressions turned to terror. They would have, no doubt, turned to run, but Phelan was already moving in a blur of speed toward them.

To the young druid, it looked as though the soldiers were moving in slow motion. He noticed with only casual interest that the cloak was gone and his arms were bulging with muscle and covered with hair. His fingers were tipped with sharp, black claws. Drool ran from his mouth which had distended into a fanged muzzle.

The first soldier went down grasping his torn throat without having moved to defend himself. The second soldier was able to hurl his spear with great force and accuracy, but Phelan avoided it easily without slowing his pace.

As his jaws closed on the second soldier's throat, he felt sharp pain in either side. The two remaining soldiers had thrust their spear tips deeply into Phelan's sides from opposite directions. He surged backward convulsively, and the two soldiers were thrown to the ground leaving their spears in Phelan's sides.

Pain was present, but it seemed distant and unimportant. Phelan yanked the spears free, and great gouts of blood ran from the wounds. After only seconds, however, the blood flow stopped, and the wounds began to knit closed.

As Phelan looked in wonder at the miraculous healing, the soldiers ran for their lives. Three of the horses had yanked free of their tethers, but one wide-eyed mount was held fast. The faster soldier mounted and galloped away as the slower staggered after pleading piteously for help. Unfortunately for the soldier, Phelan was not feeling merciful.

After dispatching the third soldier, Phelan did not hesitate. He ran off at incredible speed in the direction of the mounted soldier. The smell of frightened horse and man were heavy in the air, and Phelan had no trouble following.

The rider kicked furiously at the horse when he saw the wolf-thing gaining rapidly, but his mount had no more speed. Phelan closed the distance and hurled himself into the air. He slammed into the soldier and dragged him from the saddle. The horse lost its footing, skidded along the ground, and was back up and running without losing appreciable speed.

Phelan would have savaged the soldier, but the man had died either from the impact with Phelan or the impact with the ground. Just to be sure, he gripped the soldiers throat and twisted until he heard a wet crack like the breaking of a sapling.

Phelan's blood was up. The Romans had taken away everything important in his life. They had done it because they were stronger, and they could do it. Well, they weren't stronger than him anymore.

He scented the wind. He caught the smell of burning oak. It would be easy to follow it back to the grove. He wondered if Glyn had somehow managed to survive. He wondered if he were misusing the sacred pelt. If Glyn was still alive, he would ask. First though, the Romans would learn about slaughter from the other perspective.

Fey Fay

Sean walked along a path in the woods behind his new house. His parents told him not to go too far, but they were pretty busy most of the time. He always made it home when he was supposed to, so they didn't monitor him very closely.

Sean had spent the first ten years of his life living in a suburb of Pittsburgh, so the move to rural New Hampshire was pretty dramatic. He liked it, though. Life was brighter and cleaner and quieter. He'd always been bookish and introspective, and something about the woods in the morning relaxed him. This was especially important today because, in just a short while, he was going to start his first day at a new school.

The sunlight came through the canopy of trees in shimmering bars of gold, but the deep green pockets of shadow were still cool and damp. The smell that arose as his sneakers trod upon rich, dark soil or ancient brown pine needles was heavy and musky, but a soft breeze mixed in a light sweetness.

The breeze also brought a strange clanking sound to Sean's ears. He didn't have much time before the bus would arrive, but his curiosity got the better of him, and he went to investigate the sound.

About twenty yards down the path, Sean saw a black, iron animal trap flopping around on the ground. It couldn't go beyond a certain point because it was firmly anchored with a stake and chain. The strangeness of the scene impressed itself upon Sean, but his curiosity and his ten-year-old's willingness to accept strangeness pushed him closer.

The movement of the trap became more frantic as he approached, and he saw a flickering of color. The movement slowed by degrees, and in less than a minute, it all but stopped. Where the flickering had been lay a tiny girl with her leg caught in the trap. She was eight inches tall and had long, black hair. She wore a green and brown shift that looked shiny like satin. The most amazing aspect of her appearance, however, was her wings. They were the long, transparent double wings of a dragonfly. They twitched pathetically, but she was clearly too exhausted to move.

She looked frightened, but there was also a sad resignation in her face that made Sean feel strangely guilty. "What happened to you?" he asked then realized how stupid that sounded. She hid her face from him.

Sean knelt down beside her. "Let's see what we can do here," he said in a soft, quiet voice. She still didn't look at him. The springs of the trap were very strong, but he was able to pry the jaws apart. It was then that he saw that the trap had burned her as well as crushed and lacerated her calf.

She still didn't move, and Sean feared that she may have died. He gently picked her up. She weighed nearly nothing, but Sean felt a pulsing energy travel up his arms. She stirred weakly in his hands, and she finally looked into his face.

She didn't move her mouth, but Sean heard her voice none-the-less. "The Oak, please." The voice wasn't high or tiny as he would have expected. It was full and rich. She gestured weakly to a giant oak about twenty feet away.

Sean walked gingerly, trying not to jostle his little passenger. "Place me on the lowest limb," she said. He lifted her up onto a low, fat branch. She wobbled, and he held his hands to catch her if she fell. "Thank you," she said.

No sooner had Sean taken a backward step away from the tree than shimmering winged little people flew out of the surrounding forest. Four or five of them bore the injured girl away.

Sean looked at the palms of his hands where he felt the tackiness of the girl's drying blood and saw it soaking into his skin. The stains looked like bruises on his palms, but the discoloration faded away in moments.

Sean heard a heavy diesel engine downshifting away in the distance. He darted back in the direction of his house. Just as he was entering his back yard, he heard the bus blowing its horn. He came around the side of the house waving his arms. The bus, which had begun to move forward, stopped, and the door swung open.

Sean felt a pleasant tingling sensation all through his body, and colors seemed brighter, and sounds and smells seemed clearer. The half hour bus ride to school was full of fascinating sensory observations. He knew that a boy sitting across the aisle from him had eaten a corn muffin and a hardboiled egg for breakfast. He could hear something in the bus's engine that sounded faintly like a typewriter. And one of the high school girls had used makeup to cover a bruise on her cheek. He thought that she'd done a good job, but he just noticed the subtle difference in tones.

Sean found his classroom. His teacher was young and blond and pretty, and she smiled sweetly at him when he arrived. He stowed his things in the coatroom and took one of the twenty-five or so desks in the classroom.

He sat watching and listening to the other students chattering. They'd known each other for years, and he was the new kid. He was confident that he'd make friends soon enough, though.

He started when he saw a dark-haired boy who shimmered and flickered. It reminded him of when the tiny girl in the trap couldn't stay invisible anymore. Sean rubbed his eyes with the heels of his hands. The boy retained a smudged sort of an aura, a bruised purple-black outline.

The shimmering boy was whispering quietly to a sullen looking redheaded boy and pointing at a little, quiet boy in a *Star Wars* t-shirt. Sean didn't like how mad the redhead looked and how mean the dark-haired boy looked. His curiosity overcame his sense of caution, though, and he made his way over to the pair and held out his hand. "Hey, my name is Sean."

The two boys didn't speak, but the shimmering boy inhaled deeply, his nostrils flaring. He closed his eyes for a moment and rolled his tongue around inside his mouth as though he could taste something. When he opened his eyes, he looked at Sean with more interest. Before either could say anything, the teacher asked everyone to be seated.

Sean paid special attention at role call and learned that the redhead was named Kenny and the shimmering boy was Simon. Simon was also new to the school.

A fight broke out on the playground during recess. Kenny beat up the little, quiet boy. When a couple of male teachers were dragging Kenny into the school, he kept bellowing, "Make him take back what he said about me!"

Kenny was sent home, and his classmates whispered about it all day. Kenny had always been a bit blustery and swaggered around the playground like the king of the elementary school, but he had never really hurt anyone before.

Sean kept an eye on Simon, and during social studies, he witnessed something he could only think of as magic. Sean sat in the back row of desks. Simon sat one seat up and to the right. What Sean saw reminded him of hologram pictures, the kind in which the picture changes according to the angle from which it is observed. There was always a middle space in which he could see both images. It was like that with Simon. One image showed Simon sitting quietly and attentively at his desk. The other showed him moving about and making gestures.

Simon's attention was focused upon a boy named Johnny Spaulding. Johnny had the shoulders of a young man and smelled a little like cow manure. He sat in the front row.

When Simon made a flicking gesture, Johnny's hair above his ear went forward as though moved by an invisible hand, and Johnny grabbed his ear. Johnny turned back and glared at Tim, the boy who sat behind him. Tim looked thoroughly intimidated.

Simon made a poking gesture, and Johnny jerked forward in his seat. He twisted around and yelled, "Cut it out!"

Tim squealed, "I didn't do nothin'!" He shrank back in his seat and raised his arms defensively.

Miss O'Connor rushed over to the desks and asked in a quiet, serious voice, "What is the problem with the two of you?"

Neither spoke.

"I've had all the action I care to have today."

Just as Miss O'Connor turned her back, Simon made a pinching gesture. Johnny howled in pain and rage. Leaping up, he knocked his own desk over and clouted Tim on the side of the head with a wild haymaker. Tim and his desk both toppled to the floor. The class erupted into chaos.

Johnny was sent home. Tim was taken to the doctor's office to make sure that he didn't have a concussion. The principal came to the classroom himself to walk Miss O'Connor to his office, and teachers with planning periods watched the class through the end of the day. The kids thought that Miss O'Connor was nice, and they feared she would be fired because she was a new teacher who had two serious fights on her first day of school.

Sean felt extremely angry at Simon for wrecking everything for no reason. It was stupid and mean, and the chaos went completely against Sean's ordered nature. He also felt fear because Simon was obviously not normal and might not even be human.

Sean's anger won out, and he confronted Simon on the sidewalk in front of the school. "I saw what you did, and it was rotten," Sean growled puffing his chest up like a rooster.

Simon inhaled again. "You smell of fay, but you're not one." He waited calmly for Sean to continue.

"If you don't quit making people fight, I'll beat you up." Sean felt angry enough to do it too.

Simon smirked and said, "Really?" Simon then made a poking gesture in Sean's direction, and though Sean was three feet away from the finger, he felt a horrible burning pain in his shoulder. He gasped and pressed his hand to the spot.

Simon casually walked around and continued on his way.

Sean felt a steadily increasing anxiety as he rode the bus toward home. Who could he tell? He was smart enough to know that adults would never believe in a magical monster who looked like a ten-year-old kid. Telling other kids didn't seem any better. Even if they believed him, what could they do that he couldn't? He could see. . . sort of. . . what Simon was because of the fairy blood he'd gotten on his hand. Simon said he smelled like fay, and Sean knew that fay was just an old-fashioned way to say fairy.

An idea struck him, and he felt just a tiny glimmer of hope.

Sean dashed from the bus and dropped his backpack on the front porch of his house. He didn't even set foot inside, though, before running into the woods. He found the place where he'd freed the fairy that morning. Once there, however, he didn't know what to do. "Hello," he called. "I'm Sean from this morning."

The woods remained quiet, unnaturally so. He waited for what seemed an eternity but was only a few minutes. Sean began to lose heart.

If he had been a less confident person, he may have begun to question the reality of the morning's events.

"There's a kid in my school, but he's not really a kid. He says he knows you guys. He hurts people with magic, I think. They're some kind of tricks anyway." Silence followed.

"I need your help to stop him. I don't think anyone else can." Nothing.

Sean felt so angry at Simon's pointless meanness. He was just wrecking things for no reason. It was like kids who broke toys or scribbled on the desks with ink or clogged the toilet with paper towels, but this was much worse. People were getting hurt and Miss O'Conner might get fired.

He spoke little to his parents that night, but they were wrapped up in concerns of their own. He ate little and went to bed early where he mostly stared at the ceiling.

He still wasn't truly asleep at midnight, only dozing. That's when he heard something. He couldn't identify it at first, but when it came again, he recognized the opening of his window.

Sean scrambled from his bed getting a little tangled in the sheets. He scooped up his old T-ball bat from under his bed and faced the window. A shimmery, green-brown smudge entered and perched on his dresser.

Sean watched in the glow of his night light the smudge form itself into the winged, dark-haired, fairy girl. She smiled.

"Do not fear, Sean," she said in her unlikely big-person voice. "I have come to give what aid I may."

"Why didn't you help me today in the woods?" Sean couldn't keep all of the petulance out of his voice.

"We are forbidden to interact with humans. In the past, associations with humans have caused the fay many problems, so the ruling was made by the high court. I am low in the hierarchy of fay, and I must, at least openly, abide by the rules. I am here now."

Sean spoke quickly, a note of agitation rising in his voice. "There is this kid in my class who does things that no one else can see. He makes people so mad that they fight, and my teacher might get in trouble, and everybody is kind of scared. Somebody's got to stop him!"

"My blood has changed you," the fairy said gently. "You will see what others cannot. Fairies cast a glamour or veil, so they can move among humans. Those with more. . . potency. . . can even cause humans to see things which are not really there."

Sean looked frightened. "So how do I stop Simon? I'm not magical!" His feeling of desperation began to grow again.

The fairy held her hands out, palms downward, in a calming gesture. "Some of the fay are extremely powerful, godlike. Others, like myself, are relatively powerless. All of us are vulnerable, however." She hesitated for a moment. "I would feel a betrayer of my people if the things that I am about to tell you were not already a part of your people's written lore."

They sat up talking and planning for some time.

The next morning, Sean repeatedly checked his pockets and backpack to be sure that he had all that he needed. His heart beat a tattoo as his bus pulled in front of the school. He wiped his sweaty palms on his jeans for the twentieth time and stood up to exit the bus.

Sean hoped he could deal with Simon before the school day started because he feared the trouble that Simon could create throughout another whole day. He also wondered what Simon would do now that he knew Sean could really see him.

Just then, Sean saw Simon coming down the sidewalk, stepping onto school property. Sean ran to meet him. Simon stopped and watched as Sean approached.

"Well, what can I do for you, child?" Simon asked. He looked amused like a cat with a dazed mouse between his paws.

"So, you're just a plain old goblin, huh?" Sean asked trying to sound calm and cool.

The goblin calling himself Simon took a step back as though Sean had lunged at him. "What?" he spat. "How did you. . ." His brow grew heavy, and his lips lifted from his teeth.

"Yeah, I hear that goblins are kind of wimpy," Sean went on. "That's why they pick on little kids so often."

Simon looked like he was about to explode. His face turned red and his whole body trembled. Before he could do anything, however, Sean took a step backward and threw a handful of rice onto the sidewalk. Simon looked down at the rice and then up at Sean with an almost comical look of shock on his face. Then, he knelt down and began to pick up and count each piece of rice.

A big, grateful grin appeared on Sean's face. He quickly unslung his backpack and took out a large bag of salt. While Simon was busy picking up the rice at an alarmingly efficient pace, Sean made a circle around him by pouring the salt out onto the sidewalk.

Sean completed the circle only moments before Simon picked up the last grain of rice. He then hurled himself at Sean, snarling in rage. Simon bounced off the invisible barrier created by the salt and then bounced from the back side of the circle.

Sean smiled because he thought that Simon looked a little like a pinball. Simon saw the smile and flew into an even greater rage. The smudgy glamour that had partially affected Sean's eyes fell away, and he saw a horrible, wizened, black creature with orange eyes that glowed like embers. It snarled, "What now, boy?"

Sean reached into his backpack. Simon looked nervous, not knowing what else Sean may have in store. Sean brought out a short, heavy length of black chain. It was a part of an old, cast iron chandelier that his dad had purchased but never hung up. Simon looked terrified. He gasped, "Cold iron!"

Sean approached with the chain. Simon trembled like a cornered animal. The salt circle was small enough that Simon had no real room in which to maneuver, so when Sean tossed the chain, the creature had nowhere to go. The chain draped itself over one of Simon's shoulders like a bandolier, and the creature went to his knees. Simple contact with the chain seemed to make Simon weak and dazed.

Sean quickly circled the creature and padlocked the chain, so it wouldn't fall off.

"What now?" the creature whispered.

Sean dragged his foot through the salt circle, breaking it.

Just then, a half-dozen, smudgy auras flitted from a small stand of trees. Five of them went to Simon. He disappeared replaced by a purple-black aura. They all moved off down the sidewalk and away from school.

The sixth smudge approached Sean and turned into the fairy he had rescued. She hovered before him, her wings beating with a soft buzz. She smiled but looked a little sad. "Thank you for your help, Sean," she said.

"I'm sorry if I got you in trouble for talking to me," Sean said.

"The fay are not unaware of modern times. The tricksters are not tolerated as they once were because they endanger all of our people." She paused looking mildly chagrined. "I was reprimanded for being unmindful enough to be caught in the iron trap and for speaking with you last night. But your strength of character has shown the value of our relationship. If you wish, we may be friends."

"Awesome!" Sean said.

"You may call me Ceilia," she said and somehow managed to curtsey even though her feet didn't touch the ground.

The warning bell rang in the school. Sean said, "See ya," and ran toward the school.

If anyone had been looking at that little patch of sidewalk, Sean would have appeared seemingly out of nowhere. He was happy. He'd just made his first friend in New Hampshire.

Super V

Detective George Kelly approached the girl. She sat in the back of the squad car of the first officers on the scene, but the door was left open. A bruise was beginning to darken her cheek, and there was some blood at the corner of her mouth. She stared dazedly at the back of the headrest in front of her.

When she heard his footsteps, she looked up at Kelly, and she actually smiled. She winced at the movement of the injured cheek but continued smiling non-the-less. There was a frightened bravery in the expression that made Kelly's heart soften toward the young woman. Her hair was thick, black, and lustrous, and it hung well past her shoulders. Her skin was the color of dark roast coffee with one cream. Her eyes were dark, almond shaped, and glistening with unshed tears. Despite the bruise and obvious signs of strain, she was exceptionally attractive.

"Ms. Rosario Ling?" Kelly asked.

"Call me Rosie," she said in a voice stronger than he expected.

Kelly looked at a leather notebook. "Rosie, the account you gave to the officers who first arrived on the scene is. . . a little strange. Maybe you can clarify a few things for me."

Rosie smiled lopsidedly again and said, "Nothing has changed since then, but I'll tell the story again if you need me to." She dabbed at her eyes with a tissue, took a deep breath, and visibly marshaled her resources

Kelly said, "You say that you were accosted by five men, but there are only four bodies accounted for."

Rosie's face tightened, and Kelly feared that she might cry. She kept control, however, and said, "Yeah, he took the other one with him."

"You mean that the man in black who rescued you took the fifth man away?"

"Yes," she said.

Kelly asked, "How?"

"He just carried the guy under one arm." She seemed to gain a little more strength by describing the actions of her rescuer.

Kelly flipped through pages of the notebook. "You said that all of your assailants were full-grown men."

Rosie held up a hand, so Kelly would stop his line of questioning. "Like I said before, he carried the guy under his arm." She hopped out of the car and winced at the movement. She walked to the mouth of the alley. When Kelly came up beside her, she gestured. "Then, he jumped up to that fire escape."

Kelly said, "But that's fifteen feet up."

Rosie continued, "Then, he jumped to that fire escape over there." She pointed at another fire escape on a perpendicular wall. She paused and glanced over at Kelly. When he didn't respond, she said, "That looks like about ten feet over and about ten feet up."

"You realize that it's impossible for a human to jump those distances, especially while encumbered with a full-grown man."

Rosie shrugged. "You asked me what I saw. Possible or impossible has nothing to do with it."

Kelly looked at her levelly.

She said, "Take me to the hospital. Check my blood for illicit substances. I saw what I saw. Some super-guy saved me from . . . something terrible. He's a hero."

Kelly sighed. "This guy killed at least four men."

Rosie's look managed to be defiant and vulnerable at the same time. "Would you rather that my body was being carted away to the morgue?"

He put his hand on her shoulder and looked directly into her exotic, dark eyes. "I'm glad that you're alive and well, but I have a job to do."

She said, "You seem like a nice person, officer, but I hope you never catch him and that he kills every dirt bag in this city."

As Kelly walked back to his car, he thought about the case. He'd given Rosie a hard time about her account of the "super-guy," but hers was the third similar occurrence in a month. It seemed unlikely that a Jewish grandmother, an out-of-work welder, and an extremely attractive college girl would all share the same delusion. By some miracle, the newspapers had not focused on these particular crimes, but it was only a matter of time. This one's high body count was bound to get attention.

The vigilante was described by witnesses as wearing a full, black body suit with a full-face mask "like Spiderman's." Over the body suit he wore a long, black coat. The man was witnessed doing things which were humanly impossible. The grandmother claimed that the man leaped from the roof of a five-story building, landed gracefully, and saved her from a pair of muggers. The welder claimed that the man was shot four times in the chest by a gangbanger with a 9 mm. In each of the cases, the man in the black costume left the scene, effortlessly carrying one of the thwarted criminals away.

Kelly felt like he'd fallen into an episode of *Kolchak*. This was some weird shit. He wished he had some credible resources. There were enough crazies on the internet to keep him chasing his tail until the end of time. He had no idea how to proceed. On the other hand, Rosie made a good point about her mystery rescuer. He preyed upon violent criminals and protected their potential victims. Kelly had sworn to uphold the law, but this guy really did seem to be performing a service.

The story hit the headlines the next day: "Mystery Vigilante Saves Co-Ed." Now that reporters were on the scent, Kelly thought that they would connect the most recent event to the previous ones, and there would be a media circus. He wondered if the vigilante would lay low because of the media coverage or if his activities would escalate.

When Kelly entered the station, a uniformed officer named Helenowski asked, "Hey Kelly, did you catch Batman yet? If you need someone to ride up to Wayne Manor with you, I'll tag along."

"Sure," Kelly answered. "Maybe I should ask Commissioner Gordon to tell him to tone it down, huh."

Kelly divided his efforts among his open cases, but his mind kept wandering back to the "super-guy." He knew that he was supposed to catch him, but a strange feeling of gratitude kept creeping into Kelly's thoughts. The guy more than likely saved the lives of three citizens. Rosie's lopsided, brave smile and her hope that the vigilante would stay at large had impressed themselves upon him.

Because he could think of nothing else to do that night, Kelly drove around the neighborhoods where the vigilante had been spotted. He thought it would be a waste of time, but it was better than more "internet research." There certainly were some whack jobs out there in cyberspace. He felt too agitated to sit still anyway.

He had left his unmarked cruiser at the station and was tooling around in his personal vehicle, a ten-year-old, faded red Subaru Impreza. He thought that it wouldn't draw much attention in shabby neighborhoods, but it still had lots of pep.

His police radio was turned low, but his heart jumped when he heard the call for units only two blocks away from his location. Shots were fired. He downshifted and let out the clutch too fast. The tires squawked, the engine roared, and he was at the address in moments.

Before he exited his car, he heard the gunfire. He climbed on the brakes and leaped from the door with his Browning High-Power in his hand. He had almost reached the corner when he saw a body flying through the air. There was no arc. The trajectory was straight and level as though the man had been shot from a canon. He struck the brick wall of a store across the street with a wet snap.

Kelly hesitated for only a moment. When he rounded the corner, he was dumbstruck by what he saw. The costumed vigilante was a dark blur moving among gangsters with guns. Kelly wasn't sure if the man in black was moving too fast to be hit or if he wasn't bothered by the bullets.

Kelly threw himself to the ground to avoid being struck by another flying street thug. His gun flew from his hand. The thug struck discarded packing crates which exploded in a shower of wooden fragments. The thug did not move, but Kelly instantly scrabbled for his weapon. He was just reaching for his gun when he heard the slide of a shotgun click-clack as someone behind him racked a round into the chamber.

The vigilante leaped beyond the thirty feet which separated him from Kelly and landed between Kelly and the man with the shotgun. The weapon roared. The vigilante staggered backward narrowly missing Kelly. Kelly rolled and fired three times at the gangster holding the shotgun. The grouping was tight in the center of the man's chest, and he slumped to the ground.

Following the gunfire, the little side-street was silent save for the ringing in Kelly's ears. He turned to locate the vigilante, half expecting him to be gone. The man in black lay perfectly still. Kelly stood and looked at the body and saw that one of the wooden shards had pierced him through the back and protruded from the center of his chest. He had fallen on it when he lost his footing.

Kelly knelt next to the vigilante and removed the mask. He gasped when he saw that the vigilante's eyes were bright and alert. The man's chest was completely still. Kelly felt the man's face, and it was cold to the touch.

The vigilante smiled, and Kelly saw that his canine teeth were abnormally long and sharp. Dark, thick blood leaked from the corners of his mouth. He said in a tight, breathy voice, "A little help, please?"

Kelly's mouth hung open for a few seconds. Then he said, "But you're a killer."

The vigilante said, "You too." His eyes shifted to the body with three of Kelly's bullets in its chest.

"Are you a vampire?" Kelly asked and couldn't believe that those words had actually come out of his mouth.

"I didn't kill anyone who didn't have it coming," the vigilante said. "Look," he said. "I won't stay in jail long, anyway. Or the morgue either."

"What?" Kelly asked.

The vigilante smiled again. "Get a load of this. I'm dead!" The man let his mouth go slack and his eyes turned glassy. Kelly had already noted his lack of respiration and the coldness of his skin. He also guessed that the heart, with a shard of wood through it, wasn't beating either. Anyone would think him a corpse.

In the distance, Kelly heard sirens.

Once again, the vigilante was alert. "Time to choose," he said to Kelly.

Kelly hesitated only for a moment and decided to follow his gut. He'd wrestle with his conscience later. "What do I need to do?"

"Just get this piece of wood out of my heart."

Kelly said, "You need to tone it down. If you keep causing such mayhem, you'll be impossible to ignore."

"Yes, Officer."

Kelly straddled the vigilante, stepped on the crate pieces underneath his body, squatted down, gripped his shoulders, and lifted with all of the strength in his legs. There was a wet, sucking sound, and the wooden shard and the man parted company.

Kelly saw flashing red and blue lights coming from around the corner. He turned toward them and held his badge up above his head. He said, "Let me do the talking." When he heard no response, he turned back to the vigilante and found that he was no longer in sight.

He heard Helenowski's voice say, "What the hell happened here?"

Helenowski and another uniformed officer approached with their guns in their hands. "What are you doing here, detective?"

Kelly's mind whirled with possible lies. He decided to tell the truth, leaving out his conversation with the vigilante and his decision to set him free. He hoped that he wouldn't regret his choice. He saw Rosie's lopsided smile in his mind, and he felt surer.

"You guys won't believe this," he said to the patrolmen. "I saw this guy for myself."

Raven and the Thugs at Lizzie's Diner

James Raven sat at the counter of Lizzie's, a run-of-the-mill roadside diner near Laramie, Wyoming. Lizzie, herself, came over to offer him more coffee. Middle age had not robbed her beauty though laugh lines had turned into wrinkles, her dark hair had picked up some gray, and her hips had broadened.

"I guess I'll take one more before I go," he said. His voice was surprisingly free of a discernible accent. It was surprising because he looked like he was sent from central casting: the handsome, Native-American lead, not so baby-faced as Adam Beach and not so craggy as Wes Studi.

He wore old Levis, cowboy boots, and a blue chambray shirt. His hair was glossy black and hung to his shoulders. He knew that he was fitting a stereotype, but he liked the look, so he went with it. He wasn't really Native-American, but then again, he wasn't really human either.

He liked Lizzie's, largely because he liked Lizzie. There was nothing special about the food, and the clientele was hit-or-miss: there were good, salt-of-the-earth, working-class patrons, but there were also plenty of ignorant rednecks.

A pickup truck entered the parking lot and parked crookedly across two spaces. Raven could sense the aggression emanating from the occupants before they got out. He knew there were three young men in it, and they were spoiling for a fight. He might just indulge them. He was feeling contrary. It was about time for him to move on anyway. A man who didn't physically age couldn't stay anywhere long. He had lived here for too many years.

Raven smelled the whiskey before they even opened the door to the diner. He thought it was Crown Royal. The fumes emanating from their pores would probably be apparent even to normal humans. He looked at his watch and noted that it was just shy of one in the afternoon.

They swaggered in with insolence bordering on defiance. They didn't even make it to a booth before they spotted him.

"Hey, Chief! How!" a blocky, red-haired man said raising a hand in mock salute. His face was red with drink, and his eyes were glassy. He almost stumbled as he danced in a circle chanting, "Hey how are ya. Hey how are ya. Hey how are ya."

Conversation in the diner stopped. The patrons were actively not looking at Raven or the newcomers.

"Hey, it's last of the Mohicans!" called out the weasel-faced man who followed Red.

Raven spun his stool so that he faced the men. "The Mohicans were in the Northeast. Around here you have Cheyenne, Crow, Lakota. . ."

"Shut up, Injun Joe!" said the third man. He was dark haired and dark skinned, and his black t-shirt strained against gym-muscle.

Raven paused only for a moment. "If Injun Joe were a real guy, which he wasn't, he probably would have been part of the Illinois Confederation. Maybe Kaskaskia or Cahokia. . ."

"Hey!" Black T shouted. "I told you to shut up!"

Raven smiled, "Or what?"

Lizzie approached nervously and said, "Hey guys. Take it easy, okay."

Raven said to her, "We were just discussing Native culture." He smiled encouragingly at Lizzie.

He would be sorry to leave. He really did like his casual chats with Lizzie. She would no doubt begin to wonder why he had no gray in his hair and why his face was still unlined after so many years. I was time.

Raven knew that he was too old to engage in fisticuffs with dumb thugs. The human condition would not change. Each generation would spawn a new batch. Despite understanding this, he generally found satisfaction in meting out justice. Maybe it would be more honest to say he took out his frustrations.

"Gentlemen, I believe that our discussion is making Lizzie nervous," Raven said in a casual voice. "We should probably discontinue or relocate."

Red and Weasel exchanged glances. It was obvious that they were not expecting such a casual response. They clearly wanted to see fear or at least agitation. Black T stared hard at Raven, his jaw muscles bunching. Finally, however, he waved a hand dismissively to indicate that Raven was not worth his effort.

The tension in the dinner lessened markedly.

Raven felt a wave of disappointment. They had backed down, but he wanted to pound on them. He knew, as an ancient creature of myth and folklore, that he should be all Zen and whatnot, but his vast experience didn't always translate to his actions.

Raven inhaled dramatically. He smiled and pointed at Black T. "I smell Shoshone."

Black T's mouth fell open.

Raven chuckled. "I'm guessing that your great grandma was from the Wind River Rez."

Black T rose from his seat. The cords in his neck stood out like cables. "Liar!" he shouted.

Raven chuckled. "You're a self-hater."

Black T lunged. In the blink of an eye, Raven stood, planted his feet, and threw a punch that used the muscles of his hips, back, and shoulder. Raven's fist connected squarely with Black T's solar plexus. The force of the punch combined with Black T's forward momentum knocked Black T off his feet. He lay writhing on the floor and gasping, trying to replace the air that had been forced from his lungs.

Red and Weasel stared slack-jawed.

Raven said, "Maybe you should help your friend to find a different place for lunch."

Raven saw indecision flicker across their eyes. Fight or flight. Ultimately, their bravery was lacking. They pulled Black T to his feet. He was still making harsh gasping sounds, but he was able to walk with help.

After the truck pulled out of the lot, Lizzie said, "Jim, that didn't need to happen."

"I know," he said. The guilt he felt was amplified by the silence of the other patrons and the weight of their eyes on him. All of the millennia of his existence had not entirely removed the darker aspects of his nature it seemed.

Raven paid for his lunch with a hundred-dollar bill and said, "Keep the change." He would miss Lizzie.

Raven walked out the door and rounded a corner so that he was not visible from the diner windows. He leaped into the air, and a large, black bird flew into the afternoon sky.

Paranormal Christmas

Liam fitted the Santa beard into place. With his cheeks rouged and wearing the beard, he looked quite natural, except for the eyes, of course. The intense blueness of them was obviously not natural, but when he put on the round, wire-rimmed glasses with the blue tint, this was remedied too.

Liam loved Christmas just as he had loved it when he was alive. He used to wonder if the damned should celebrate the birth of Christ, but after a hundred years or so, he decided to just go with it. After all, he wasn't struck by lightning or anything. He even went to mass at St. Patrick's. The first time he expected his blood to boil and his skin to blister, but when he found that they didn't, he decided to make a yearly practice of it.

This struck Liam as strange because he'd seen his kind driven away by crosses, sparks flying and holy power rolling in waves. He'd also seen holy water leave smoking craters in the flesh of the undead. Liam wasn't brave enough to touch the holy water at the back of St. Pat's, nor was he going to take communion, but crossing the threshold of the church and listening to hymns and prayers was actually quite pleasant.

Liam had only begun dressing as Santa recently, in the last fifty years or so. It was great to spend so much time close to humanity in well-lighted rooms without having to beguile people into thinking he was normal. In the dark, he could pass for human. Under the bright lights, the chalk-white of his skin and the intensity of his eyes would give him away in a minute.

Liam exited his dressing room and strode toward Santa's Village in the Mid-Town Mall. He heard squeals of delight from children who saw him. He felt such warmth in his old, old heart every time he heard, "Mommy! It's Santa!"

He took his seat on the soft chair covered in red velvet. Jessica, the photographer, said, "Hello, Santa. Are you ready to see these nice boys and girls?" She winked broadly at him.

"Of course. Of course," Liam said in his stage voice. "Ho ho ho."

A little boy was brought to Liam by his pretty, blonde mother. Liam lifted the boy onto his knee and said, "Ho ho ho, what would you like for Christmas?"

This went on for hours, and Liam loved every minute of it. The feelings of warmth and love and optimism were a balm for the centuries of pain and suffering he had witnessed.

When a little boy approached him all by himself, however, Liam started in surprise. The boy looked, on the surface, like a cute, dark-haired child, but Liam could see a smudgy, purple aura around him. Liam squinted his eyes, bringing up his preternatural sight. In place of the little boy, he saw a black, wizened creature with glowing, orange eyes. A goblin.

Liam did not want to let on that anything was amiss, so he said, "Ho ho ho, what do you want for Christmas?"

The goblin gave Liam an almost comic look of surprise, but he cautiously climbed onto Santa's lap. The goblin whispered, "What's your game, bloodsucker?"

Liam said, "I just really like Christmas."

The goblin looked at him steadily with his weird, orange eyes and said, "Huh, me too."

Sidhe

James was returning from the storeroom of his father's general store to the back lot when he saw the crate slide awkwardly from the supply wagon. His father's muscles bunched as he tried to get a handhold, but it was a lost cause. James was a blur of motion, and he was at his father's side in moments. Together, they wrestled the crate back onto the wagon bed.

Kevin McBride was the only father James had ever known, but it was clear that they didn't share blood. McBride was six-feet-tall, red-haired, and thickly muscled. James was just over five feet tall, despite being fifteen years old, and he was dark-haired and slightly built.

McBride kneaded the muscles of his lower back and said, "I will certainly feel that tomorrow." His brow furrowed in thought. "Where did you come from, anyway? I thought you were inside."

"I was. You're just getting slow in your age." He patted his father's brawny shoulder. "Why don't we carry the crate together."

James bore his half of the load without great strain as the two headed to the storeroom. After carefully lowering their burden, McBride said, "I will never understand how such a slender lad is so damn strong. You could at least pretend to work harder at it."

Father and son entered the main store where Mr. Andrews measured out salt for a customer. Andrews was a tall thin man who made up for the loss of hair on the top of his head by wearing a huge handlebar mustache.

After the customer had gone, James said to Andrews, "So, Jeanie brought you those wonderful biscuits for lunch. Are you going to share?"

Andrews smiled and said, "I always ask for extra just for you." He began to turn back to his work when he asked, "How did you know Jeanie brought my lunch? It's usually Mrs. Andrews."

James shrugged. "Lucky guess."

The truth was that Jeanie smelled different than Mrs. Andrews. There was a familial similarity, but the two scents were distinctive. James maintained a simpler life by keeping that sort of thing to himself. He was abundantly aware that he was. . . not like other people, but he tried to be as normal as possible around others. Of course, his parents and Mr. Andrews knew him too well and for too long to completely deceive them.

Almost fourteen years earlier, James had been found wandering naked down the main street of town. People guessed that he was about

114

eighteen months old by his size. Constable Kevin McBride, who was also part owner of the general store, took in the child. After a long search for the child's real parents, McBride and his wife adopted the little boy, named him James, and raised him as their own.

The town hall bell began ringing frantically. It was too early and too wild for the noon bell. Something was wrong.

McBride grabbed his gun belt from behind the counter and strapped it on. To Andrews he said, "Bob, you'll need to mind the store." To James he asked, "You coming?"

McBride and James found the town hall door standing open. Willy Milford stood jittery and fidgeting just inside the entrance next to the bell rope. His eyes were wide, and his face was pale and sweaty. When he saw James and his father come through the door, his mouth worked, but no sound came out.

"What's the matter Willy?" McBride asked.

"You gotta come, Constable!" Willy wailed. "It's horrible!"

Willy's eyes began to roll up, and he would have fallen if James had not gotten an arm around him. Even though Willy was a big boy of thirteen, James had no trouble holding him up and moving him to a nearby bench.

McBride slapped Willy lightly on the cheeks until he began to come around. James went to get a cup of water. When he returned, he heard Willy say, "It's Suzie. It's horrible." He said those same two sentences over and over again, and James wondered if he had been saying them since he regained consciousness.

James pushed the cup into Willy's hand, and, thankfully, Willy stopped talking and slurped loudly.

McBride sighed and seemed to accept that he wouldn't get any clear information out of Willy. He and James each took one of Willy's arms and moved him back toward the general store. A small crowd whose curiosity had brought them to the Town Hall followed the trio down the street.

"Is there anything we can do, Constable?" asked a large bearded man wearing the leather apron of a blacksmith.

"I don't know yet, Mark," McBride said. "I'll call on you if I need you."

"What happened?" One of the crowd asked.

McBride stopped and turned to address the crowd. "I don't know anything yet. You should all go about your business, and I'll find you if I need you."

He waited until they dispersed before continuing on. Willy moved like a clockwork, his face flaccid and expressionless.

Rich, the driver who brought supplies to the store, was just getting ready to leave.

"Rich," McBride called. "Do you have to head back to the city right away?"

Rich craned his neck around to look at the small group. "No, Kevin. I've got a couple of hours. I was going to The Lion, but that can wait."

"Will you take us to the Milford farm?" McBride asked.

"I guess this has to do with the bell," Rich said.

"Yep."

"Climb in," Rich said. "You'll have to tell me the way. I don't know it."

The Milford farm was only two miles from the town center, so it didn't take the men long to arrive. Ben Milford stood at the end of his long driveway.

Ben Milford was a wiry, leathery looking man who wore farmer's overalls, and a wide brimmed, shapeless, brown felt hat. He nodded at McBride, vaulted into the wagon, and said, "She's at the barn."

The barn was large and well-cared-for. Mitch, Ben's ten-year-old son, stood to the side. He looked as pale and sick as his big brother had at the Town Hall.

McBride, James, Rich, and Ben made their way to where Mitch stood. Ben put an arm around the boy and said, "Your brother is in the wagon. Why don't you boys go back to the house and sit with your mother."

Wordlessly, Mitch did what he was told.

Suzie had been the oldest of the Milford children. She was sixteen two months earlier, and she would get no older. She was obviously killed where she was. The blood spray on the side of the barn and the pool of blood in which she lay proved that. But the method of killing was unclear.

Ben said, "At first I thought it was an animal like the one that's been killing the livestock lately. Then, I saw this. He motioned with a gnarled, callused hand to a single, bloody boot print in the short, matted grass. "That's bigger than my boots or my boys'."

As James looked at the horrible scene, something strange happened. He felt a tingle like a static charge at the back of his neck just at the base of his skull. A shimmery mist the color of old ivory seemed to hang over the murder scene. One tendril of mist led across the field and disappeared over a rise.

James looked from the mist to the faces of the other men. None seemed to be aware of what he was seeing or feeling. They just continued with their examination of the area and questions and answers.

"That Stephen Pike has been coming around, trying to win my Suzie over, but she had no interest in courtin' him," Ben said. "That boy always seemed a little strange to me, but I don't think he coulda done anything like this."

McBride asked, "Did they argue or fight recently?"

"Nope. He ain't been around for a week or longer," Ben said shaking his head. "I just can't think of anyone who would do something like this to my Suzie." Ben's voice began to quaver, but he clamped it down. "She never done nothin' to hurt anyone."

McBride put his hand on Ben's shoulder. "I'll have Doc come over and get her. There's nothing else we can do here."

McBride turned to James and Rich. "I'm going to go over to the Pike place, James. I want you to measure that shoe print. Then, ride back to town with Rich and send Doc Shaw out to get the body." He said to Rich, "Is that okay, Rich."

"Yeah, I can wait around a bit. I have to go back that way anyhow."

"After that, James, I need you to hitch up our wagon and bring it out to the Pike place."

"Okay, Dad."

Rich and James rode back to town in silence. James had always known that he was faster and stronger than other people. He could see farther and smell and hear more. To say that he wasn't curious about it would be untrue. He had come to accept it, though. Whatever happened at the Milford farm, however, was of a far greater magnitude. Now, he knew that he would have to somehow find out who he really was.

One thing he knew for sure was that Stephen Pike did not kill Suzie. He'd caught a scent at the scene unlike anything he'd smelled before. Something about it was familiar, but he couldn't place it. Stephen, though, had not been there.

After James spoke to Dr. Shaw and dropped off the shoe print measurements at the constable's office, he went back to the store to tell Mr. Andrews that he and his father would be occupied most of the day.

"It's been awful slow in here today, James. I think I can manage on my own," Andrews said. "What happened out there anyway?"

"I probably shouldn't say anything until I check it out with Dad," James said. He felt a little sheepish keeping something back from Mr. Andrews. He had known him all his life, but his father had specific rules about constable business.

James saw McBride sitting on the front steps with Stephen Pike when he reached the Pike place. Pike's father Angus stood on the lawn looking pale and shocked.

James set the brake and jumped down from the wagon. "What's going on, Dad?"

"We're taking Stephen back to town," McBride said.

"Could he possibly do something like that?" said Angus in a dreamy voice. He didn't seem to be addressing anyone in particular.

Stephen answered the question, anyway. "I didn't do it, Pa." He looked at the bloody rag McBride held in his hands. "I have no idea how that got in my room."

By way of explanation, McBride said to James, "It's a piece of Suzie's dress, and it's covered in blood."

"Why would I keep something like that, constable? It don't make sense," wailed Stephen.

"We'll get this sorted out, Stephen. We've got to do it in town. It's for your own safety as well as anything else," McBride said in a soothing voice.

"You don't let anything happen to my boy, constable," said Angus. "He's a good boy. You know he didn't do this as well as I do."

"I've got to follow the evidence. He'll be safe at the constable's station. Nothing will happen to him on my watch."

The ride back to town was nearly silent. McBride, James, and Stephen were lost in their own thoughts. Occasionally, Stephen made a hitching sound in his throat as though he were fighting back a sob. The only other sounds were the rattling of the wagon and the clop of the horse's hooves.

A crowd came out to follow the wagon when it came into town. The people asked many questions, but McBride put them off. Stephen was locked in a cell, and one of Mark's apprentices from the smithy sat with him and had instructions to ring the bell if there was any trouble.

McBride decided to go back to the Pike place to interview each of the family members and learn what he could, but James asked to stay behind.

"Dad, you know that sometimes I get feelings." James paused to give his father time to respond. McBride nodded. "I'd like to help. I think I can, but I'd need to work alone. It's one of those things."

McBride looked at his adopted son. He knew James was different. He'd understood that from the beginning, but through some silent communication, they had agreed not to actually speak about it aloud.

"Okay," said McBride. "You know that I'll need proof, not just your. . . hunches."

"Thanks," said James. "Stephen didn't do it."

"I know," said McBride.

James took off toward the Milford farm at a sprint. Even though the distance was two miles, he never slowed. He was only slightly winded when he reached the bloody, matted grass where Suzie had lain a short time ago.

Things looked normal to his eyes, as normal as a murder scene can look at least. He didn't know how to recreate the phenomenon which had occurred that morning. It had happened naturally, by accident.

He would have tried to concentrate, but he didn't know on what to focus. He inhaled through his nose, held the breath, and breathed it out slowly. He repeated this pattern several times. As he relaxed, his eyes began to unfocus. At one moment, the world looked normal, and at the next moment, his head buzzed, and he saw the ivory ground mist.

James inhaled and memorized the killer's smell as well as the quality of the buzz. Maybe the buzz would be the same every time, but he wouldn't know until he sensed another one. It didn't take him long to realize that the tendril of ground mist that moved across the field was a trail, so he followed it.

James picked up more and more speed as he found that maintaining his special vision took no effort, and the trail was simple to follow. His loping run took him to the Pike farm. He felt a moment of doubt. Could Stephen be the killer? He saw, however, that the trail continued back toward town.

It led to the home of Mark, the blacksmith. That was strange because the scent James had memorized was not Mark's. Neither was the scent from either of Mark's apprentices. Did they have a recent boarder or a visitor? James thought that unlikely. In a town of this size, any outsider was remarkable, and he had not noticed any new faces or scents.

James squeezed his eyes shut and willed away his special sight. Whatever patterns he might see with it might be insightful, or they might muddle his normal perceptions. Until he practiced more, he didn't want to overuse it.

He came up with an excuse to visit Mark as he climbed the short steps to the front door. When the big man came to the door, Mark said, "Dad was wondering if he might be able to use your boys again tomorrow at the jail. He really likes someone to be with the prisoners at all times."

"Of course, I'll help out Kevin. Those apprentices of mine are both coming along in their skills. A little time away from the smithy is probably good for them." Mark stepped back from the door and said, "Why don't you come inside for a bit."

The cottage was small and neat. Mark was a bachelor but seemed able to do the necessary housekeeping chores for himself. His boots were off and his shirt was half unbuttoned. On the kitchen table sat a jug of dark ale and a stein.

"Would you like some of Matthew's ale? This batch is especially good," he said. Mark meant to gesture toward the stein, but he misjudged the distance and knocked it to the floor.

"Damn," he whispered. Then, he smiled at Mark and said, "At least it was mostly empty. I have a whole cabinet of steins."

James wanted more time to learn something, anything really, so he said, "Sure, I'll have one. Dad loves Matthew's ale."

"Give me a moment to clean this mess," Mark said, and he bent over to pick up the largest shards of the broken stein.

As Mark bent, a medallion fell from inside his shirt to hang from its golden chain. On it, a horrid, fanged face was represented in bas relief, and rubies glinted in its eyes. Something happened then that was similar to the head buzz and ground mist at the murder site. It was similar but far more intense.

The ruby eyes flared, and James saw a nimbus of scarlet energy around Mark. What James had felt as a buzz earlier in the day was a grinding pressure on his skull. He had no idea if anyone else would be able to see this, but Mark, or whatever it was, was certainly aware of being seen.

The Mark-thing's head snapped up, and it snarled at James. James had known Mark for his whole life, and he knew without a doubt that this was not Mark. It smelled a little like Mark but also of something else, something burned and corrupt. It was the smell from the murder site.

The thing's head tilted to the side. Its nostrils flared, and then it hissed something that sounded like, "Shee!"

James was up in the blink of an eye and balanced on the balls of his feet. There was only about five feet between the two of them. He did not want to retreat, however, for fear that the movement would invite attack.

The thing spoke in a harsh, grating voice. "Well well well. A changeling."

It moved with impossible speed, striking with black talons which appeared in an instant.

If James had moved any slower, he would have been disemboweled. As it was, he suffered four deep, painful gashes across his chest and stomach which left his shirt in tatters. His backward spring carried him eight feet into Mark's living room.

The thing did not pause for a moment. It lunged forward, claws outstretched.

James grabbed a heavy wooden chair and brought it around in a tight arch to crash into the thing's head and upper body. It staggered.

James dropped the chair and snatched at the medallion. He caught hold of it. It held for a moment, but one of the links let go, and James stumbled backward with the hellish thing in his hand.

He felt heat and pressure climb from his hand to his forearm. He tried to let it go, but his fingers were locked into place. The power moved past his elbow. He frantically tried to will it back, but he didn't know how to do that. Heat and pressure reached his shoulder, and he felt sure that he was lost. Whatever had happened to Mark would happen to him.

How was he supposed to fight when he didn't know what to do? Using these powers just happened by accident. Things just happened.

His mind snapped back to his experiences at the Milford farm earlier in the day. The first time, exposure to the residue from this creature seemed to wake up a part of him which he didn't even know existed. On the second occasion, he was able to recreate the experience by calming himself and letting the power surface naturally.

It took every ounce of his faith in himself and his hunch to stop fighting. He had been trying to hold back the power like a dam holds back water. Now, he became like a rock in the middle of a river, and the power flowed around him like water flows past the rock. He felt the rage and corruption skimming over his surface now. He sensed it wanting to leap the distance between him and Mark, but the thing needed contact. He was sure of it.

Unable to gain purchase into James, the power flowed back into the medallion. James was able to unclench his fingers, and it fell to the floor with the thud of a much heavier object.

Mark lay unconscious on the floor, but he breathed regularly.

James needed his father.

James and McBride led Mark, confused and tired, to the jail in the town hall. Stephen asked what was going on, but the constable put him off until morning.

James and McBride sat in the constable's office in silence. James wasn't sure what to say or how to begin it. He had never lied to his father in any major way, but he had kept a good deal from him. Should he lay everything out for him? He couldn't think of any partial truth or outright lie that would keep Stephen and Mark from the hangman's noose. The community would demand that someone be punished.

"Dad, Mark killed Suzie Milford and probably the livestock before her, but it wasn't his fault. . ." James looked up when his father didn't respond. McBride waited patiently.

"Whatever you do, don't touch this with your bare skin." James reached into his pocket and brought out the medallion wrapped in a red handkerchief. He opened the little bundle, and the two of them stared at the evil face and the little ruby eyes. "This did it somehow," James said. "I don't know when or where Mark got it, but when I tore it off his neck, he seemed himself again." He paused. "And I was almost something else."

"But you fought it," said McBride.

"Yeah, I could do that somehow." James made a decision at that point. "Dad, what's a changeling?"

McBride's eyebrows rose. "Well, my parents told stories from the old country. Some of them involved changelings. They're fairies who are substituted for human children. They usually create all kinds of mischief before vanishing back to the land of fairies."

James looked at his hands. "It also called me 'shee.'"

McBride nodded, hearing something which he expected. What he said sounded like "theenee shee," but James learned that it was spelled "daoine sidhe." McBride said, "It means people under the hills. It's one of the many ways to refer to fairies."

Father and son sat in silence for a long time. The sky grew dark. Finally, James said, "I can't stay."

McBride said, "I know."

Totem

Waya holds the silver cup in his hands, but the pale skinned ones cannot see him. He pleads with them that they not bring the fire. Someone had taken the pretty cup, yes, but they did not realize that the theft would be felt so strongly by the white soldiers.

The soldiers throw flaming brands into huts and onto corn fields. There is barely enough food as it is, and the soldiers will take what they want as well. All of Aquascogic burns to ashes.

Chief Wingina tells the people to refuse the pale soldiers food. The soldiers grow angry, and they fire their guns. Wingina tries to escape, but the one called Nugent pursues him and returns from the forest carrying Wingina's head by its long blood-matted hair.

Waya cried out and sat up on his mat of straw and animal skins. Perspiration covered his aging body and glistened in the light of the dying fire. The dream had come again. It had become a nightly occurrence in recent weeks, leaving him shaken and trembling every time.

Waya dreamed of the pale-skinned ones. They were not so few now; they were as numerous as the stars, and they would crush his people into the earth. Waya had removed himself from his tribe, the Croatan. The spirits moved him in ways that he did not often understand. They spoke to him and gave him signs. One night they told him that he must leave his village and live separately from all. It was after the first pale-skinned ones, the soldiers, had burned Aquascogoc and stolen food and eventually killed Wingina.

His people said that the new settlers were different. They had women and children, and they planned to make their own food and not steal from the Croatan. Maybe they were different, Waya thought, but they would still kill. Only a season ago, the settlers had slaughtered a group of Croatans, thinking them to be Roanoacs. His people were forgiving and believed that it was all a dreadful mistake. Waya's pleas fell on deaf ears. "Leave the killing white people to themselves," he had said. "They are stupid and weak. They will die on their own."

Waya stared long into the fire. He loved his people. He had had a good life with them, but they had become foolish. They insisted on helping the very people who would destroy them.

His eyes had become damp as he looked into the fire. He was a healer, but to help his people, he felt he must rid them of the whites for their own good.

Waya shook off the last of the dream and carefully moved across his cave in the dim light of the fire. He retrieved his medicine pouch and drew forth a wolf totem carved from dense black wood. It held powerful magic, and Waya feared it, but the spirits had spoken to him. He had faith that the spirits were guiding him, and he began the ceremony.

Mathias couldn't sleep. He wasn't sure why, but he felt a slight pressure in his bladder and decided to use it as an excuse to get up. The autumn night was a chill, so he put on a coat before going outside to relieve himself. His mother and father and little brother slept soundly, snuggled deeply under their thick blankets.

The brisk air of the night sent sleep even farther away than it had been, and Mathias remained outside even when his business was completed. The stars twinkled brightly in the clear indigo sky, and the crisp air invigorated him and cleared his thoughts. He enjoyed the play of his thoughts as his mind traveled of its own volition.

The population of the settlement was low, and Mathias dreamed of the day when the supply ships would come and bring new settlers. Hopefully pretty, young girls would be in plenty. There were now no girls near his age. They were either married or too young.

Mathias imagined a ship full of girls who would all clamor for his attentions. He would show them the island, and they would be grateful.

Suddenly, the hair on Mathias's neck stood up, and he froze in place. Off to his left and down a slight rise, he saw something luminescent moving through the moonlight. They looked like men, but they made no sound traveling over crisp autumn leaves.

They moved closer, but their direction would bring them past Mathias, not directly to him. They moved quickly, hunched over like animals. He heard them sniffing at the ground and went absolutely still. These creatures were not men, but they were not beasts either.

The creatures seemed to catch and cast back the moonlight in an eerie glow. They were dressed like the Indians in summer and had intricate patterns tattooed or branded onto their skin. From the neck up, though, they were wolves. The creatures did not wear masks. Mathias could see their noses wrinkle as they sniffed at the ground, and their breath clouded out before them. On one in particular, he saw the moonlight glisten on the drool dripping from its mouth.

Mathias knew he should shout to warn the others. He wished he could reach the village first, but he knew he couldn't outpace them.

Mostly, he was just terrified. If he hadn't just voided his bladder, he would have at the sight of the wolf creatures.

Like a gunshot, the silence of the night was shattered by the howling, barking noise of the creatures. Shortly after, he heard a scream and then another and another. Men's voices shouted. The meeting bell clanged. Three musket reports cracked.

The sounds of battle loosened Mathias's feet from the ground, but God forgive him, he didn't run toward the town, he ran away. He ran blindly, without thought or skill. He crashed through brush, breaking limbs and scattering leaves. His breath seemed to tear at his throat as he gulped it down and gasped it out. Sweat burned the crisscross patterns of small cuts on his face and hands that he'd gotten in his mad run. Finally, he tripped over a root on the dark forest floor and went sprawling.

He heard nothing in the forest around him, not a bird or a frog or an insect. Only his own whistling breath and the pulse pounding in his ears broke the silence. He sensed them coming though. They moved silently, but he knew they were bearing down on him. Although a part of him wanted to wait and let them end his terror, his desire to live drove him to stand on his shaky limbs and continue.

He had lost his sense of direction, but in the distance, he saw a pale glow. For a moment, he feared it was the glow of his pursuers, but he saw that it was the Atlantic. A breeze from the ocean dried the sweat on his brow but didn't comfort him. His skin went tacky, and he shivered uncontrollably.

Mathias's heart nearly slammed through his ribcage when the strange barking howls erupted behind him. He turned to see three of the wolf creatures. They crouched, their tongues lolling out of blood foamed muzzles. Steam rose from their heated bodies. Their chests heaved from their exertions or from their excitement.

Mathias bolted, operating wholly on instinct and adrenaline. He made for the water. He must have surprised the creatures if they could be surprised at all.

Just as he dove into the surf, he felt a burning pain on his back. The water was numbing cold, but he thrashed farther and farther out. The frustrated barking howls of the creatures encouraged him more than they terrified him. They wouldn't follow him. He could see them milling around the shore. The others began to arrive.

Mathias knew his back was injured. At first the cold water numbed the pain, but the salt from the ocean water worked in to start the burning anew. The creatures were not moving away as he had hoped. They took up positions on the beach, watching him. They could easily wait him out. He would freeze if he didn't get out of the water and dried soon.

Mathias had begun to feel groggy and thought of how freezing to death would be preferable to being torn apart by monsters. He started, though, when he saw a human figure appear on the shore.

An old Indian's was visible in the moonlight, but he was not luminescent like the others. It appeared to Mathias that the Indian was talking to the creatures. One of them gestured in his direction. The old man strained to see but shook his head in frustration.

The figures waited on the beach, but after a while, the Indian gathered all of the creatures around him. He held something dark above his head. The creatures looked at it and vanished into the moonlight. Mathias gasped in amazement but did not fail to notice that the old man put the object in a pouch at his waist.

Mathias's teeth began to chatter, and something about the feel of his heartbeat made him nervous. Still the old man sat on the shore waiting for him, no doubt with a knife in his hand.

Mathias decided that he had to do something. Remaining still would mean his death. He hoped that the old man couldn't actually see him from his place on the shore, or his efforts would probably prove worthless.

He moved parallel to the shore, trying not to go into the water deeper than his chest. Progress was slow. Not only was he moving through deep water, but the cold also seemed to be stiffening his joints. A burning feeling cut through the numbness he had felt before. A terrible image of exiting the water to find his limbs all blackened and cracking entered his mind.

He hoped he had gone far enough when he decided that he must get to shore or die. The strength seemed to be draining out of Mathias as he neared the shore. Would he make it, or would he be food for the sea life of the coast? He finally pitched headlong onto the damp sand of a beach. He tried to crawl to the cover of trees farther inland, but the darkness overtook him.

Mathias woke because he felt too hot. He lay too close to a fire, and he was covered in heavy animal skins. He tried to struggle free, but a gentle, firm hand held him down. His vision wouldn't focus properly, but he thought he saw dark figures on the other side of the fire. He stopped trying to rise or throw off the covers, and he heard a man speak. "Sleep now, Englishman."

When Mathias woke again, the sun was just coming over the horizon. He was hot, and his hands and feet throbbed painfully. He felt shock and prudish embarrassment when he realized that he was naked under the bearskins covering him.

An Indian sat cross-legged before the fire, and six others still lay under their blankets. The Indian prodded at some embers and said without turning to Mathias, "The black skin did not start. You have only the red skin."

Mathias pushed himself up into a sitting position and winced at the pain in his hands. He supposed it could be far worse and was thankful that it wasn't.

The Indian stood up in one fluid motion. He picked up Mathias's clothes from their place by the fire and brought them over to him. He squatted next to Mathias and handed him the clothes. "I am Achak. Bad magic happened in your village last night."

Mathias started up, mindless of his lack of clothing or the pain in his extremities. The part of his mind that remembered wolf creatures had shut down, and now all of the memories came flooding back. Anguish over the loss of his family and friends, terror at the thought that monsters do exist, and shame at his own flight from danger. His face contorted with the passing emotions. He buried his face in his hands but did not weep. Something held the tears back.

Achak read some of Mathias's thoughts and said, "If you did not flee, you would now be dead." Mathias trembled and couldn't seem to get a breath, but he forced himself to be calm. His heart rate slowed, and his clenched muscles relaxed, and he was able to fill his lungs with air. He concentrated on breathing for what felt like a long time.

Achak walked to the edge of the clearing where he could see the Atlantic stretching on forever. He didn't know what to do, but he had to help this boy. He knew the magic unleashed on the boy's people, and it frightened him. He thought he knew who was responsible. The boy could probably let him know for sure. What would he do about it?

"How did you learn our language?" Mathias asked, as he struggled into his pants while favoring his stinging hands.

Achak faced him and smiled. "I am. . ." He paused for a moment, looking for the proper word. "cousins with Manteo. He speaks your words well."

"So do you," Mathias said.

Achak nodded, accepting the compliment.

The others began to stir and rub the sleep from their eyes. They spoke to each other in their own tongue and seemed to agree on something. They exchanged words with Achak and drifted away into the trees.

"Are you Croatan?" asked Mathias.

Achak nodded.

"Do you know who did this to my village?" Mathias asked.

Achak sighed and thought for a while before responding. "Tell me what you saw."

Mathias shuddered, but he described his memories of the previous night as closely as he could. Achak made encouraging sounds or gestures when he had trouble in his account and asks for clarification at certain points.

When Mathias had finished, Achak spoke. "The old man is Waya. He was medicine man for the Croatan, but his heart was bad for whites. The Croatan would not attack the whites, so he left to live alone and get more sick in his heart."

Mathias looked down at his reddened hands and said, "I guess the mistake at Dasamonguepeuc didn't help his sick heart any?"

Achak said, "No," and stood silently for a long time. "Waya has strong magic, and we would stop him even if you were dead. What he did is forbidden."

Mathias nodded. "Where does he live?"

"There," Achak said, gesturing vaguely westward. "We will follow him."

The others returned with fish a short while later, and they cooked them over the fire for their breakfast. They broke camp afterward and headed west.

Mathias's feet ached a bit inside his boots but not as badly as he feared. The night before, one of the creatures had only scratched his back shallowly, but the rubbing of his shirt and jacket tatters against the wound irritated him terribly.

The group traveled all day. The Indians in front knew well how to track, but Waya must have expected pursuit for he left many false trails. Much of the time was spent backtracking and looking for the place at which Waya had secretly changed direction. It was dusk before they reached Waya's cave, and he waited for them quietly at the entrance.

Waya spoke to the Indians in their own language. Achak seemed to be the spokesman. The words became heated, and Achak gestured repeatedly toward Mathias. Waya leveled an especially baleful glare at him.

Achak grabbed Waya's arm, but the old man threw him off with surprising strength. He then thrust a finger toward Mathias. Achak shouted a sharp word at Waya and began to advance again.

Waya thrust his hand into his medicine pouch and brought out the wolf totem. Achak stepped back and shielded his face. The totem flared for a moment, and the wolf-creatures appeared before everyone's eyes, wavery and translucent one moment and solid the next.

The Croatans surrounded Mathias without a word. Knives and war clubs seemed to appear in their hands instantly. They kept their backs to Mathias to form a bristling perimeter.

The creatures advanced. They swung their razor claws menacingly, but they wouldn't strike the Croatans. They circled and slavered and growled and barked, but they would not attack.

Achak and Waya began to shout at each other, probably about the stalemate. Waya gestured madly at Mathias, but Achak shook his head and shouted.

Livid with frustration, Waya thrust the totem skyward again. It flashed. The creatures looked at it and at Waya. He shouted at them and gestured at Mathias and the Croatan alike.

The creatures charged, yellow gleaming teeth bared. Achak acted instantly, but not to fight the creatures. His knife flashed through the air in precise tight circles and buried itself in Waya's chest. The totem flew from his fingers as the old man crumpled to the ground.

The creatures slammed into the Croatans, but the Indians moved like cats, twisting and turning away from the snapping teeth and grasping claws of the monsters.

Mathias dove for the totem. He missed it, and it bounced away. He scrambled after it. He felt blinding pain as two-inch-long teeth sank into his right calf.

The Indian weapons frustrated the creatures but seemed to cause them little damage or pain. The creatures raged, and the Indians tried to survive.

Mathias's fingers closed on the small wooden statue, and suddenly, the teeth were gone. He rolled over to see the creature, its chest heaving, crouched over him. The creature was not looking at him though. It stared at the totem, transfixed.

Mathias looked to find his friends and saw them locked in combat and fading fast. He struggled to his feet. His head swam, but he refused to fall. Not knowing what else to do, he thrust the statue skyward and shouted, "Hey!"

All of the creatures froze, then slowly turned toward Mathias. Their eyes never strayed from the totem. "Go away, back to where you came from!" he said loudly and strongly. Mathias doubted that they spoke English, but they vanished instantly and without a trace.

Achak limped over to Mathias who still held the totem in the air. "You have saved us," he said solemnly.

Mathias lowered his arm. "You wouldn't have needed saving if not for me."

Achak nodded.

Mathias handed the totem to Achak. "I don't know what to do with this. Do you?"

Achak took the statue to the mouth of the cave where he found a flat rock. He placed the totem there, and with another rock, crushed it to fragments.

Mathias wept long and hard for all he had lost. The Indians waited patiently. None had died, but all were wounded to some degree. They tended their hurts and Mathias's when he began to recover from his sobbing.

They went back to the village where Mathias gathered his things. All were surprised at the absence of bodies. The creatures must have spirited them away. Blood spatters were visible, and the ground was churned in various places indicating struggles. In a short time, the rain and the snow would remove these signs as well.

Governor White had told the colonists before he returned to England that if they were to change locations, they should leave a sign. Mathias was the last of them, but he thought he should follow instructions. He would live with the Croatans. With his knife, he carved "Croatoan" into one of the palisades and he left with them.

Guardian

Mark walked down the sidewalk with his bulging backpack slung over his shoulders. The pack was heavy, and the muscles of his thin back screamed with the weight of it. He had so much work to make up after his sickness that his Spring Break wouldn't be much of a break at all. He didn't want his GPA spoiled. As a freshman, he felt that his grades really counted now.

Mark had always been thin, but after suffering through a case of mono, he had gotten even thinner. He still wasn't really over it, but at least he wasn't contagious anymore. He should have asked his mother to pick him up from school, but he hated to be a bother. He wished now that he had been a little more selfish.

He dropped his backpack on the sidewalk at his feet. His back muscles throbbed and pulsed, and he groaned as the knots slowly loosened. He figured that he had come about halfway home, but that still left over four suburban blocks.

As he stood in the sun recovering, he felt the dampness of sweat at his armpits and the small of his back. The chain of his new necklace chaffed at the back of his neck, and he considered taking it off, but something in the weight of it comforted him. It had been his uncle's.

The last time his family had visited his grandparents, his grandmother had a box she had taken from the attic. It contained all manner of sentimental items, the kind of things grandparents keep. He guessed that his grandparents were getting to an age when they wanted to pass things on to people who truly wanted them.

His mother had actually cried when she saw the necklace. It was a sterling silver yin-yang. Back in the seventies, his uncle loved martial arts movies and actually studied Kung fu. He was only fifteen when he died in a car accident with a friend who had just gotten his license. Mark's mother had been devastated because the two of them were so close. She made a big deal about passing on something so significant to him.

The necklace did feel significant to him. He thought it was probably just because his mother made such a fuss, but still, he did find it comforting.

Mark continued on his way, determined to make it all of the way home before putting the bag down again. Unfortunately, his body was not equal to the task. He had barely made another block before he had to stop again.

Mark lived in a middle-class, suburban neighborhood. It was about as safe as any place could be, but predators could be found anywhere. An overhang of dark trees on Hannah Street was where the bad kids spent much of their time.

He didn't want to stop anywhere near that area, but his aching back demanded that he rest. He dropped the pack to the ground and stood in the shade waiting for the throb in his back to subside. He only needed a few minutes, and he would move on. Unfortunately, he didn't even have that long.

Mark didn't see Kenny Borden and company right away. He smelled the smoke from their cigarettes. He considered leaving his backpack and making a run for it, but he hesitated. He couldn't stand to see books destroyed, which would likely happen, and his Walkman was in there somewhere. Anyway, the mono had left him so weak that even this bunch of smokers could catch him.

"Hey, twerp! Whacha doin' in our spot?" said Kenny as he swaggered toward Mark. Kenny was overgrown and fat in a hard way. He had dropped out of school the year before at the age of sixteen, and his cronies would likely follow his example when they became old enough.

"I was only stopping for a minute," Mark said. "I'll go now."

"No, you ain't," Kenny said with a malicious smile twisting his face. "You ain't goin' nowhere."

A detached part of Mark's mind wanted to make him say, ". . . aren't going anywhere." Mostly, though, he was just scared.

Mark knew that Kenny would squash him like a bug, but he had no idea what to do about it. He couldn't fight, and he couldn't run. He sighed. Mark decided that if he was going to get the snot kicked out of him anyway, he would go down swinging.

Mark charged and threw himself at Kenny. Kenny, slow by nature and caught totally off guard, was able to make no defense. Mark's small fist struck him in the well-padded stomach, and Kenny grunted more in surprise than pain. The real damage came from the toe of Mark's tennis shoe as it connected solidly with Kenny's kneecap.

Kenny bellowed like a bull and crumpled to the ground. Kenny's cronies stood dumbfounded. They had never seen anyone effectively fight back, and they couldn't figure out what to do.

Mark had a window of opportunity, but amazed at his own desperate success, he hesitated again. He looked up from Kenny writhing on the ground in time to see the others advancing on him. He turned to run but made only a few steps before he felt hands gripping his shoulders and throwing him to the ground. He landed badly, and the breath was knocked from his lungs.

As Mark lay gasping, Kenny was able to get to his feet. He kept most of his weight on one leg and glared down at Mark. "You are so gonna get creamed, twerp."

Mark couldn't respond because he was still trying to make his lungs take air. Speaking wouldn't have helped anyway. The Kenny Bordens of the world had no reason for doing the things they did. They were too stupid and mean to be reasoned with. They hurt other people simply because they could.

"That kid sure is wimpy," said a voice next to Kenny.

Kenny turned toward the voice and winced at the inadvertent pressure on his wounded knee. A tall, well-muscled kid stood next to him looking down at Mark. He wore a white T-shirt, khakis, and a denim jacket. His hair was long and blond and in no particular style. His hands were thrust deep into his pockets.

Everyone stared at the newcomer who had appeared completely unnoticed. Their eyes flitted around the group to see if everyone was as surprised as they.

"Who the hell are you?" Kenny spat once he regained his composure.

The kid grinned widely and ignored the question. "God, how pathetic would the punks who beat up this kid be?"

Kenny glowered and said, "Are you some kind of a wise guy or somethin'?"

The kid never stopped grinning and said, "Yes."

"You want your head kicked in or somethin'?" Kenny roared. He was mad, but something about this kid made him nervous.

"Or somethin'," the kid said.

By this time Mark had caught his breath and followed the exchange with a growing sense of hope. The kid taunting Kenny wasn't all that big, but he had a confidence and competence in the way he carried himself that made him seem big.

"Why don't you take a hike?" Kenny said trying to sound in control, but he was clearly unnerved.

"Why don't you take a hike?" the kid said back in a good-humored voice.

Kenny could not intimidate the kid, and he didn't want to lose face in front of his friends, so he took a swing. It might have caused terrible destruction if it had actually hit anything but air.

The kid's hands flew out of his pockets as he stepped back out of the range of Kenny's fist. The kid stepped in again with a bouncing motion, gave Kenny a double jab in the solar plexus, and bounced away again. Kenny gasped for breath and staggered on his wounded leg. He tried to cry out, but he couldn't get enough air into his lungs.

The kid stepped in again and neatly punched Kenny in the nose. The punch looked casual almost gentle, but Kenny's nose began leaking blood almost immediately. He stumbled to the ground making whistling sounds like a boiling tea pot. There was real fear in his eyes.

The kid stood over him smiling down. "Kind of feels like you're drowning, doesn't it? You suck in air because I knocked the wind out of you, but you're also inhaling your own blood. You won't really drown from it. . . I don't think so anyway."

The kid turned to Kenny's friends who stood with their mouths hanging open. It seemed that their minds simply couldn't grasp what they had seen.

The kid said, "So, do you boneheads want to dance, or are you going to run away? I would suggest the second choice."

Three of the larger boys looked from Kenny to the kid, and they looked at each other and nodded. They came at the kid quickly, and they fanned out so two could flank him. The expression on the kid's face was almost joyous. His smile caused the boys to pause for just a moment.

The boy on his right took a swing first. The kid sidestepped it and struck the boy's extended elbow with his left forearm. The blow didn't seem to hurt the boy much, but that combined with the momentum of the boy's own swing twisted his torso exposing his back. The kid's right fist drove into the boy's kidney. The boy crumple with a whimper.

One of the boys had gotten behind the kid and pinned his arms in a bear hug. The other boy waded in with clenched fists. The kid brought his heel down on the right instep of the boy pinning his arms. The boy's ankle bent strangely, and he howled in pain and released the kid.

The kid was not released soon enough to avoid the blow, however. His attacker's fist connected solidly with the kid's flat stomach. Mark expected to hear a whoosh of air expelled from the kid's lungs. He expected to see the kid double over and maybe even fall to the ground. Neither of those things happened.

It was even more of a surprise to the attacker than it was to Mark. The boy had felt his fist connect solidly. He'd beaten up enough people to know what to expect. In all other cases the person who was punched did not grin at him like an ape.

"Hold that pose," the kid said.

"What. . ." the boy began, but the kid's fist slamming into his nose stopped his query. The boy clapped his hands over his nose to try to stop the blood which ran out of it freely.

Kenny and his crew were either writhing on the ground or otherwise expressing a desire to leave off the fighting. Some of those who had chosen not to engage in the fight looked at their injured friends like they wanted to help, but they were too afraid to move.

The kid helped Mark up from the ground then effortlessly hitched Mark's heavy backpack over his shoulder. He waved pleasantly at Kenny and said, "See you around."

The kid set off toward Mark's house. Mark hurried to follow. The kid set a brisk pace, but unencumbered by the backpack, Mark was able to keep up.

"Hey, how do you know which way to go?" Mark asked.

The kid smiled. "Isn't this the direction you were headed?"

"Oh, right," Mark said. "What's your name?"

"George," he said.

George, the kid, whistled a tune that Mark found familiar, but he couldn't quite place it. It was happy and bouncy.

They walked side by side companionably until they reached the steps of Mark's house. George swung Mark's heavy backpack from his shoulder as though it was light as a feather. He placed it at Mark's feet.

George said, "See you around." He turned and walked away with his hands in his pockets. After a few steps, he began to whistle the bouncy tune again.

Later that evening, as Mark was helping his mother clear the supper dishes, he found himself whistling the bouncy tune. His mother looked at him strangely. She said, "Where in the world did you hear that?"

"Just from a kid I met today," Mark said. "Why?"

His mother smiled a little sadly, "Your Uncle George loved it. It's a disco song called 'Kung-fu Fighting.'"

Mark hauled his heavy backpack full of schoolbooks upstairs to his room. He was just about to start whistling the catchy tune again, but he didn't. A thought had occurred to him. Aloud he said, "George?"

Mark went to the hall closet where his mom kept old photo albums and other keepsakes. He found an old, worn, faux-leather photo album. He flipped through the pages until he found what he was looking for, something that he only remembered vaguely.

From a slightly yellowed, slightly faded photograph, his rescuer stared at him, smiling widely. A silver yin-yang necklace hung around his neck. Beneath the photo in his grandmother's neat, looping handwriting, Mark read, "George, June 1980."